WITCHWOOD

OTHER BOOKS BY TIM LUKEMAN

Rajan
Koren

WITCHWOOD

Tim Lukeman

TIMESCAPE BOOKS
Distributed by Simon and Schuster
New York

Use of the trademark TIMESCAPE is by exclusive license from
Gregory Benford, the trademark owner
SIMON AND SCHUSTER is a registered trademark
of Simon & Schuster, Inc.
Designed by Eve Kirch
Manufactured in the United States of America

1   3   5   7   9   10   8   6   4   2

Library of Congress Cataloging in Publication Data
Lukeman, Tim.
Witchwood.
Summary: Befriended by an unusual woman, Fiona
leaves the hated orphanage and goes to reside in Harrow
Hall, where she becomes aware of the perils and
responsibilities of being "marked" and embarks upon a
dangerous course of adventures.
[1. Fantasy]   I. Title.
PS3562.U465W5   1983   813'.54   [Fic]   83-4943
ISBN 0-671-47549-5

for Mimi Panitch

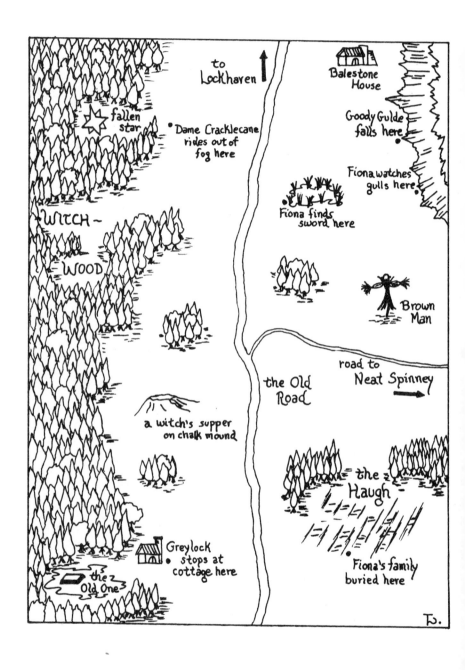

to
Lockhaven

Balestone
House

Goody Gulde
falls here

fallen
star

Dame Cracklecane
rides out of
fog here

Fiona watches
gulls here

WITCH—

WOOD

Fiona finds
sword here

Brown
Man

road to
Neat Spinney

the Old
Road

a witch's supper
on chalk mound

the
Haugh

Greylock
stops at
cottage here

the
Old One

Fiona's family
buried here

Ʇɔ.

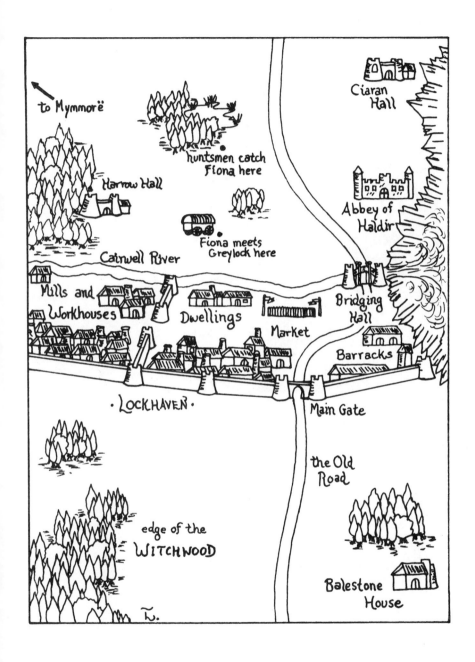

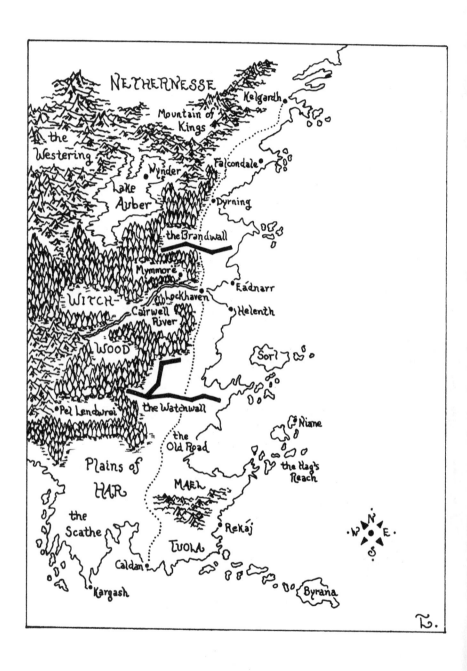

One

FIONA SULKED ALONG THE EDGE OF THE CLIFFS, ignoring the sun as it melted like brass in the evening clouds. Flocks of gulls drifted in the breeze, their wings dyed red as icicles dipped in strawberry jam. She barely remembered the taste of that childhood treat. The gulls wheeled over her head. Her pale, freckled cheeks glistened with tears, which she loathed almost as much as those who had caused them, but she was too stubborn to wipe them away. She had denied her own tears for the last few months. Tears made her feel too vulnerable now that her family was gone, but this once she indulged in them.

Why had she been sent *there* by the Law? She glanced at the gabled roof and crumbling towers of Balestone House. How she hated that place!

The orphanage was shrouded in wet moss and ivy, but the diamond panes of its windows glinted in the dying sun, making her think of unblinking eyes. She looked away from the gray walls of the orphanage. The gulls hung in the wind, just out of reach, luring her over the cliffs.

Why shouldn't she listen to them? She gazed down at the jagged rocks that shattered the gray waves into froth, tinged brown as dried blood in the sunset. It would be the simplest way to end the misery of her life.

She brushed away the motley of faded bronze leaves that clung to her kirtle, which was the rough white homespun of an indentured girl, and snorted at the temptation.

She would never give them that satisfaction! It would be better to push the others over the cliffs, especially that

Goody Gulde! She slowly rubbed her fingers together, still red and stinging from the birch rod. The dead leaves blew in her tangled hair, rustling as she combed them into the cold wind. The waiting sea churned below the cliffs. Her mouth was taut with determination.

The countless bells of the Three Towns began to toll as evening washed over the coast, turning the sea into pale gold and shadow, scattering embers through the clouds. The great lighthouse of Eádnarr was kindled, and its cannons boomed out three times. The chill, haunting cries of gulls lingered in the twilight.

Fiona reached into the pocket of her drab cloak for the ceremonial cattle goad that had been in her family for untold generations. It was made of silver, its filigree of twining vines and hawthorn leaves blackened with age. She had hidden it from the warders when she came to Balestone House, for it was the only tangible memory she had of the past...her father working in the fields, his tanned face shining with sweat, a straw in his mouth, musket and powderhorn close at hand...her mother boiling quince for jam over the brick hearth, wearing the green apron dotted with marigolds, singing a lullaby. It seemed too distant to have been real, and she tightened sore hands about the antique cattle goad before it could melt away with the rest of the past.

The plague took her parents late in the winter, and she was sent to live in the orphanage according to the inexorable Law of Lockhaven. She had been utterly miserable ever since that day.

Why did they have to die? The gulls soared within easy reach, but she ignored them. Why did it still have to hurt so much, and for so long?

Dusk was now the quiet gold and warm ash of memory, and she let it wash over the grief she sought to deny, biting her lip to hold back more unwanted tears. She had to be strong, now that she was alone, if she was to live in the world. She could not give in to weakness when there was no hand to give her the strength she needed. She would find that strength in her own heart. There was no other choice, for her childhood was gone, leaving her to make her own place in the world.

What place? She sighed wearily. I go to the workhouse each morning, and the little I earn is given to the orphanage each night, and even if some of it *is* saved for me, it can't be very much!

She looked back and smiled at the country, watching the wild ponies run through the sweet grass of the meadows, their shaggy brown manes like hay in the wind. She liked to bring them apples, and although they would bite others, they always ate calmly from her hand. She often thought that they could understand her, but that could only be the foolish wish of an awkward girl without friends.

The soft burr of her voice and the plain manners of the country were such little things, but they were enough to mark her as different inside of the orphanage, and set all of the children against her. She soon realized that she was the one red bird in their white flock. —A lot of babbling hens! She turned up her nose with disdain, recalling the taunts she had endured in the last months. They're all the same, including Deirdre! She says that she wants to be my friend, but I know better! She's one of *them!*

She and Deirdre had been taken inside the orphanage the same morning, but while she had been singled out by the other children for taunts and malicious pranks, Deirdre had become their darling. The pranks came to an end when Fiona thrashed one of the boys and knocked out three of his teeth, but that had sent her to the stable for the first of many birchings by Goody Gulde. Deirdre was presented as the example of proper conduct at Balestone House. Fiona brooded over the injustice of it all and loathed Deirdre.

She had felt some faint guilt when she recalled how she had spurned the friendship hesitantly offered by Deirdre, but any guilt was lost in the jealousy that gnawed at her heart.

It's bad enough that she's the sweetling of everyone in the orphanage. Why does she have to be so pretty? It's just not fair!

Fiona gently touched her face, as if to brush the spray of too many freckles from her cheeks, and compared her tangle of auburn hair to the kelp that floated at the bottom of the cliff. She decided that her nose was pointed as well— just like a twig! She sighed, buttoning her cloak as the evening wind grew colder. Why couldn't she look a little like her mother? Just a little would have been enough.

The only thing she truly liked about herself was her wet eyes: green as new leaves, with flecks of gold swirling deep in them. They made her feel very special, as if she had been chosen by hawks to fly in their wild, lonely company. Fiona knew it was nonsense, born of her wish to escape the taunting of the other children, but it comforted her whenever she was left out of games of Skip-the-Stone or Hunt-the-Hare. It was either that or believe they were her betters, and she would never believe that. She might be alone, but she was proud of her loneliness, for it was all that she had now.

It's been months since they made me come here. I still don't fit in, not one bit. I probably never will, no matter where they send me.

"I don't care!" she cried, startling the flock of gulls that blew like chaff in the wind. She had never intended to admit so much. "I don't care at all!"

She turned away from the sea, her hands thrust into the

deep pockets of her cloak. The wind stung her cheeks red and whipped her hair. She gazed up at the sun, whose last coals had crumbled into ashes, and lost her misery in the awakening night.

First there came the trembling sheets of white and gold mist, unfurling slowly across the darkness of the horizon, an immense sea that bobbed with numberless stars. Each swirled through the misty heavens, leaving a lazy trail of saffron or silver or cinnamon. The fixed stars shone like emeralds and gold in that vastness of haze and froth. The opulence of the heavens seemed boundless.

Then she saw the oldest moving stars, scattered through patches of darkness, all but their cores burned away in wisps of white and gold mist. There were fewer stars forming like dew in the heavens. Many of the oldest had begun to dissolve into embers and ash that fell to earth, where their remnants might be found in the shallow waters of a pond, or among rows of beans, or in the branches of an oak. Those who found the core of a fallen star might make their fortunes, for it was a honeycomb of crystal that oozed molten silver and gold. The time would come when only the fixed stars would still burn in the heavens.

Lastly came the moon, shining bitterly over an enormous swatch of starless night. Its antlered shield rose above the edge of the chalk cliffs. Fiona wanted to hurry back to the orphanage now. Holdir was hunting the heavens.

She made her way down the gentle slope of the path that led away from the cliff, wading through the heather, watching the shadow of an owl flicker over the quiet meadow. She saw the lanterns of Lockhaven burning through the branches of the apple orchard that grew between the large town and Balestone House. Dogs barked in the distance. She hiked up her kirtle and began to run.

The meadow was a blanket of fragrant clover, bounded by mossy black oaks and broom pines, with cracklecane growing in dry hollows. Pools of drowsy sweetwater, floating with mock honey, glistened icily in the silent moonlight. The wind was damp, tasting of brine and wild mint. Scarlies wheeled over the dark, rustling crown of Witchwood. Their harsh cries reminded her of the musty tales that had frightened her when she was a little girl on the farm.

She saw the white, crumbling bones in the pools of warm sweetwater, bristling with pale yellow reeds, where those who drank too deeply of their lost dreams had never awakened. A brown fox peered at her through the grass, just like the ones she used to shoot with her father's musket. She had watched the chicken coop most of the summer one year....

Fiona caught her breath. The air tasted of ginger, and ashes began to fall softly upon the clover, touching the pools of sweetwater with the hiss of quenched candles. She caught ashes on her tongue, tingling with hot ginger, and wished upon the falling star. It was all nonsense, but some part of her still believed in such childish things.

There was more ash sifting down from the night, and she imagined that the star would be scattered along the length of the country, its rich core breaking up in embers long before plummeting to the ground. It was surely a ghost star, little warmer than any common hearth.

A ghost star. —Just like me, homeless and lost! Fiona pouted, then bit her lip with disgust. She would not start brooding like that again! And she didn't really believe in wishing upon stars—

She flinched as a fiery thread of pain seared along her cheek. The air was burning with ginger, and she looked up in disbelief. The drifting ashes were shot through with silver and gold. She gently touched her cheek, watching as the core of the falling star plowed into the sweet clover at the edge of the Witchwood.

Dear Lady! She began to shiver from more than the bite of the wind. With that much gold, she could easily buy all of Balestone House!

She shook as thunder rumbled slowly in the wake of the fallen star, whipping her patched cloak about her like broken wings, and trembling black waves billowed through the field of clover. The moon was hidden by a flock of scarlies, their startled cries swept up in the cold wind that gusted across the meadow, following the thunder into the night. Fiona drew her cloak tight, her ears ringing, and carefully licked the ash from her sullen lips.

I could buy all of Balestone House! She smiled coldly at the thought of the fallen star, and her mouth grew dry. I could do anything at all with that much gold!

She hesitated, remembering the old wives' tales haunting the dark wood, but the unexpected hope of ruling her own life was stronger than her fears. Anyway, it hadn't fallen *inside* of the Witchwood! It might be her only chance to do what *she* wanted to do with her life!

She glanced back at the orphanage, brushing a damp lock of hair from her face, and made up her mind. Just wait until she returned with all of that gold! She clenched her aching fingers with bitter satisfaction. It would be worth any risk to see their faces then!

A torrent of dead leaves blew out of the night, crusted with icy brine, and slapped her eager face. She cried out in sudden fear, clawing the leaves from her clammy cheeks. Her heart drummed furiously as she tried to catch her breath.

Mother would have called this an omen. Fiona shuddered as she combed the dead, crackling leaves out of her hair with stiff fingers. Father...would he have called me greedy?

"I don't care," she muttered, wading across the pool of

sweetwater, her toes wriggling in the thick mud. She wanted more than the orphanage could give her—which is nothing at all! I don't call that greedy!

Her feet were clogged with warm mud as she stepped out of the pool. She reached down for a handful of moss and mint leaves to wipe her feet. Her groping fingers closed around metal, and she drew a bronze sword out of the dripping reeds.

It was pitted and dull, but she could still discern the filigree of alder leaves and an antlered moon cut deep in the blade, dark with verdigris. The hilt was knurled bone woven with gold beneath its shroud of muddy leaves and moss. Fiona gripped it with both hands, bit down on her lip, and chopped at a rotting log. Soggy bark flew in the bright moonlight as the blade thudded into the log. Fiona grinned with surprise and wrenched it loose, feeling like Morwenna, the heroic Marl of Ciaran.

It had been five years since the People of the Stallion Banner came riding out of the southland, clad in red deerskin and rabbit pelts, their faces darkened with woad: and it had been five years since their gathered tribes were broken asunder by the muskets and iron swords of the Three Towns.

The looters must have missed this! Fiona struggled to swing the sword back and forth, making coarse stubble of the reeds. I really should bring it with me.

She laughed at the thought, but the sword made her feel less vulnerable, and she refused to drop it back into the mud at her feet. The wind plucked at her hair. She knotted her fingers about the slippery hilt. It was heavy, but she could manage to wield it.

There were always highwaymen. Also she was too stubborn to leave the sword behind, although her arms were starting to ache with its weight—and she would simply have run away from any highwaymen. She made up her mind. The sword belonged to her now!

Beads of fog rolled like oily pearls across the meadow. Fiona slung the sword over one shoulder, staggering until she had it balanced comfortably, and stepped out of the rustling reeds. The sluggish pools of sweetwater behind her were like the ruin of a shattered honeycomb, and each breath tasted of mock honey. She trudged through the wet clover, black leaves whispering after her in the wind.

The gathering fog became damp golden haze as it washed over the crumbling star, which lay in a glade just within the Witchwood. Two oaks stood like gate pillars at the entrance to the glade, bearded with dripping moss, and the other trees were choked with brambles and holly. She walked between the brooding oaks. The mist of burning ginger blistered the roof of her mouth. The fog softly brushed her face like boneless fingers. She approached the fallen star hesitantly, the warm earth muffling her steps.

An ooze of shimmering gold dripped from the star, thick with ashes and blackened shards of crystal, bound with veins of silver that intertwined like boughs of hawthorn. The fog boiled in folds of crackling mist that smelted the soil into embers and obsidian. Fiona shielded her eyes from the glare with one hand.

"Dear Lady!" she whispered at last, sheathing the sword of pitted bronze in the ground. She stepped closer, coughing as the smoke of hot ginger seared her throat. The throbbing fire of the dying star flowed within her like sweet wine, and she stepped even closer to it. This was surely the granting of her wish!

A white falcon plunged out of the fog, and its loud cry sent her sprawling across the clover, striking her head on a jagged lump of flint. She put one hand to her brow and felt the hot stickiness of blood. She lowered her trembling hand to the ground, catching her breath, her heart thrashing like the wings of a trapped sparrow. Pale drops of sweat mingled with the blood on her brow. The lingering cry of the falcon seemed to mock her, and she glimpsed the sweep of wings like snow through the fog.

What had possessed her to come here? Fiona shivered as fog poured over her, seeding her cloak with drops of dew that burned gold in the rich blaze of the star. Her head pounded as she struggled to her feet. She realized that she stood at the edge of the dark Witchwood.

There were clumps of dead leaves sticking to her hands, but before she could brush them away, she saw blackened runes of soot and web clinging to them. She gasped and shook them away with flailing hands, wiping her fingers clean in the wet clover, choking on fear and disgust.

I was a greedy fool to come here! She crumpled to the earth upon her knees, the blood roaring loud and insistent in her ears. Why was it growing so dark?

She paled as the wind gusted through the glade, bearing with it more leaves, but it was the sound of hooves that made her stiffen with fear. Dear Lady, protect me! she beseeched the night. She bit deeply into her lip. The leaves pawed at her cloak. The hooves came closer, steady as the beating of her heart. *Clop clop clop...*

Fiona clutched at the hilt of the bronze sword, meaning to draw it from the earth, but her fingers grew limp when she saw who rode out of the fog.

The woman was clad in robes the green of moss and young beech leaves, her long black hair woven into dozens of braids pouring down her shoulders from an unbraided raven's wing of hair covered in white lace and delicate web-of-gold. A soft nimbus misted her form, as if she were cloaked in dissolving beads of moonlight, and in that quiet glow only her wide eyes could be clearly seen. They were green as mint, with clouds of wet gold in their depths. She rode with the assured grace of the Gentry.

The woman might have emerged from the songs and legends of any childhood. Fiona would not have been surprised to see Kesen Stonehelm, who had woven nettles for nine years to win the hand of Oenowë; or Lany the Cobbler, searching among rows of cabbages for his lost wits; or Roke Wyndirél, whose hawks brought vengeance for his betrayal and death upon the sons of Etarre.

"Who is this?" murmured the woman, bringing her mare to an abrupt halt before Fiona. She looked down at the girl and softly gasped in disbelief. "Lethan!"

A horseman rode out of the fog, his brown mantle folded back over russet breeches and hunting jacket. He was plainly of the Gentry. There was a fashionable lock of woven silver pinned in his black hair, which tangled under the brim of his plumed hat, but that was his only affectation. He carried a flintlock pistol by his side, along with pouches of gunpowder and lead shot. The fog wrinkled about his shoulders, and he shrugged it uneasily into the night.

"Well, what's this?" he said, drawing spectacles out of his waistcoat and setting them gently upon the knife blade of his nose. He seemed more the scholar than one of the rulers of Lockhaven. "I never expected to find a runaway girl while riding after treasure, Jennet."

Fiona grasped the bronze sword with both hands, tasting blood as she bit more deeply into her lip, and forced herself to her feet. She barely had the strength left to stand, but she pulled the sword from the earth. "You can just keep your distance!" she warned the horseman. "I can wield this!—"

"I'm not going to hurt you." He smiled, drawing back in his saddle. "Lethan is my name, the Marl of Harrow. What is yours, child?"

The woman beside him gently took his hand. "I'll speak

with her," she said, dismounting with the ease of years. "Do fetch those laggards with the wagon."

The horseman doffed his wide-brimmed hat with a wave of its black plume. "Just as you say, Jennet." He laughed, his elegant gesture rewarded by her smile, and spurred his white stallion into the fog.

"I won't hurt you either," said the woman, striding up to Fiona. "Now, would you lower that fearsome sword? We've much to discuss, my dear."

"Who are you?" demanded Fiona, shaking the lank strands of hair from her eyes. She felt warm drowsiness washing over her like honey. "What do you want?"

"I am called Dame Cracklecane," murmured the woman, her mouth crinkling softly at the corners as she smiled, brushing the dead leaves from her long braids. "I would like to help you, my dear."

Fiona gazed at her with disbelief, for Dame Cracklecane was the name of an ancient hag with warts in the puppet shows that made their way from town to town in wagons painted blue and scarlet and gaudy gold. She could not keep from giggling in spite of her fears, and she said, "That's not really your name, is it?" She frowned. "He called you Jennet."

"Lethan may call me that," Dame Cracklecane smiled, her fond voice sparkling like an icy stream. "We'll make do with Dame Cracklecane. It should serve us comfortably for now."

Fiona lowered the heavy sword, its tip digging into the ground. The smells of wet mint and hot ginger and cold sweat mingled in the fog. She wondered what she was doing here, a sword in her hand, when she could be sleeping in her warm bed at Balestone House.

"Dame Cracklecane," she said at last, rubbing the sleep from her eyes with the back of her hand. "That's an uncommon choice of names, isn't it?"

"I'm an uncommon woman, so what better than an uncommon name?" The gray fog shone like lace as it touched the nimbus that misted her form. "However, we have something very much in common, Fiona."

"How do you know my name?" whispered Fiona, raising the sword before her with aching arms. The runes carved into the blade caught the fire of the fallen star, dancing quickly as sparks. "Who are you really?"

Dame Cracklecane stretched out her hand. "I would like to be your friend," she said, and the nimbus that had cloaked her melted into the fog. Fiona could see the wrinkles under her wide eyes. "I should like you to trust me as your family trusted me, Fiona."

"You knew them?"

"Yes, my dear."

"That's easy enough to say," retorted Fiona, holding up the sword with effort, but doubt shaded her voice. "How do I know that it's the truth?"

"Your favorite lullaby was 'The Brown Wren,' you enjoy two pats of butter on your porridge, and you caught the croup when you were three years old. Do you need to hear more, or would you agree that only your family could tell me such things? It is the truth."

Fiona swallowed the lump in her throat, struggling with the memories that rose like dim ghosts. "You must have known them," she whispered, her voice cracking despite her efforts to remain calm. "What do you want of me?"

"I only want to be your friend," said Dame Cracklecane. The simplicity of her gentle words was persuasive. "There is no other reason for me to be here, Fiona."

"You didn't come out in this fog just for me," insisted Fiona, wanting to believe her words. "What about all of this gold?"

"I have no need for it, and you are welcome to claim my share with your own." She smiled at Fiona. "We did not come here to cheat you, my dear! You will be wealthy, if that is your wish, but I offer you more than wealth. I wish that you could bring yourself to trust me."

"I want to," Fiona murmured, an inexplicable longing in her voice. "I don't know what to do, don't you see? I can't even trust myself, so how could I trust you?" She struggled against the warm drowsiness that brushed her eyes, wincing as her strength bled with each throb of her brow. "I couldn't take that risk."

"My dear, you've already taken that risk by speaking of it," said Dame Cracklecane. "I know how difficult it must be for you, but there's no need to distrust me, not when we are of the same blood."

"What do you mean?"

"Look closely at me, Fiona."

"Your eyes—!"

"Yes, we both bear the Mark," said Dame Cracklecane, the softness of her voice torn away like dead leaves in the wind by an arrogance that both frightened and attracted Fiona. "I learned of it many years ago, when there was little more for me than feeding pigs and sweeping out stables." She wrinkled her nose in disdain. "I dreamed of better things, just as I am sure you have, and I found them in the Mark."

Fiona nodded, for while her deepest wish had always been to be accepted just as she was by the other children, they had rejected her from the beginning. She seldom voiced that wish these days, but it was all the more true for her unwillingness to admit it. She already felt set apart from the others, and if she could not draw closer to them, she would listen to this mysterious woman. She made up her mind and asked, "What does it mean to be marked?"

Dame Cracklecane laughed with delighted eyes. "You make it sound dreadful, and it is anything but that, my dear!" She raised her hand, glistening with beads of dew. "This is what it means."

Fiona closed her eyes as gentle fingers touched her brow with piercing warmth, like balm of honey and embers, smoothing the raw, painful gash. "What are you doing?" She opened her eyes and looked at Dame Cracklecane.

There was blood trickling along her fingers, and a burst of sparks from the smoldering star turned that blood to molten gold. The air was sweet with the fragrance of wild rose and fresh linsey. She held out her hand to Fiona.

Here was another omen for mother. Fiona slowly touched her brow. There was no wound. Mother was gone, and she must make her own choices now. Fiona would not believe in omens.

She reached out and took the waiting hand, which gently closed around hers with assuring warmth. It was easier than she had feared it would be—but she did not know what it was she had to fear. Dame Cracklecane squeezed her hand. Fiona managed to smile awkwardly at the woman.

"Now, that wasn't so bad, was it?"

"N-no, it wasn't."

She was startled by the loud creaking of a wagon, drawn by oxen, that rolled out of the gray fog. It was loaded with rough slabs of ice, still crusted with the straw and sawdust of the cellars in which they had lain since last winter. Men in the stiff leather aprons and breeches of blacksmiths walked beside the wagon, bronze digging tools in their hands, gazing about with wary eyes. Each wore his black hair in an ornate knot at the nape of his neck, clasped with weathered bone and dark gold. Runes of woad twined about their brawny arms and became alder leaves upon their brows. Scars showed like bone through the dark woad.

Scathlings! Fiona watched them dig the crumbling star out of the ground, hot ginger and molten gold streaming from jagged cracks, their faces growing filthy with ashes. What were they doing in the service of the Marl?

"Gwyn?" called Lethan, his mantle flapping like brown wings as he cantered out of the swirling fog. "Now that the wagon is here, perhaps we may return this child to Balestone House." The woman opened her mouth in dismay, but he raised one hand to forestall her words. "I know how you feel about this, but it would be best for all of us—"

"No!" Fiona said angrily, looking up at him with fierce determination. "I'm not going back to that place! You can't make me!"

He leaned forward in his saddle, his fragile spectacles dangling on the tip of his nose as he frowned at her through the fog. "You'll do as you're told!" he said firmly. "It's for your own good, child."

The condescending tone of his voice was too much for her to bear, and she shouted, "I have a name, if you care to hear it!" She turned to Dame Cracklecane. "I won't go back, no matter what he says, and I don't care if he *is* the Marl of Harrow!"

Lethan pushed his thin spectacles back to the bridge of his nose. "You are so like Elspeth," he said. "I don't wish to see you share her fate, m'lass."

"Lethan!"

"Jennet?"

Dame Cracklecane glared at him, hands on her hips. "Do you mind keeping such notions to yourself?" she said. "Fiona is coming to live with us at Harrow Hall." Fiona glanced at her in surprise. "She should learn of her heritage, and that will never happen in that gaol of an orphanage! Do you want her to go through life scrubbing floors? She deserves better than drudgery!"

He gazed at her with resignation. "You've already told her of the Mark," he said grimly, leaning from his saddle to clutch a handful of blackening leaves from a branch, which he brandished in her impassive face. "Well, have you told her of this? It's starting all over again, Gwyn!"

Fiona could see that the leaves were mottled with runes of web and soot. "What does he mean?" she asked, cringing as he flung the leaves at her feet.

Dame Cracklecane angrily shook her head. "It's nothing to trouble you, at least not for the moment," she assured the uneasy girl. "Lethan, there will be time enough to speak of this at Harrow Hall."

"Gwyn, this is the time to speak of it," insisted the Marl. "The child deserves to be told of the many perils that accompany her—gift."

"She deserves to be told of her heritage," replied Dame Cracklecane. "I never intended to dismiss its perils." Her eyes were weary green as she turned to Fiona. "You have the choice of coming with me or going your own way in the world. Lethan is right, you know. There are perils in learning the mysteries of the Mark. There are also many rewards, and the least of them is learning who you are, my dear." She smiled wanly. "How will you choose?"

Fiona considered both of them. Lethan had called her a child and treated her as one. Dame Cracklecane possessed an air of proud loneliness that reminded her of herself. There was really no choice at all for her, not while there were so many questions in her mind.

"I'll go with you." She restrained the urge to stick out her tongue at Lethan. "You don't take any disliking to that, do you, m'lord?"

He shrugged his shoulders in defeat. "Balestone House must have had its hands full with you, m'lass." He swung his stallion about, turning toward the southrons. The remnants of the fallen star were almost loaded into the wagon. Lethan took an embroidered napkin from his waistcoat and wiped the fog from his spectacles. "I won't feel safe until we're back at Harrow Hall," he said, glancing at the dark trees. "How much longer, Egil?"

"N'long, Lord Harrow." The Scathling grinned. Sweat ran down the cracked leather of his face as he and his men fought to heave the smoldering bulk of the star into the back of the wagon. "Ye'll soon be back in th' hall."

A shining billow of steam rolled around him as the star touched the slabs of ice in the wagon, hissing as it settled into notched planks of hard oak. "Well and done!" Egil said as he lifted goatskins of wine from under the wagon. "Drink up, m'lads! Ye've earned it this night!" He offered one to Lethan. "Your throat may be dusty, eh?"

"Let's be on our way," urged Lethan. He looked about as if he heard something moving through the quiet fog, drawn more by their presence than the fallen star. "We've been here too long for my liking," he muttered, fingering the oaken stock of his pistol. "There have been tales of blood offerings in the glades of the Witchwood."

Fiona saw the fear in his gray eyes, and as dead leaves flurried in the wind, she remembered the many evil legends of the dark wood. She disliked the way he looked at her, as if blaming her for his growing fears. "Please don't stare at me that way!" she snapped, knotting the hem of her cloak in her hands. "I didn't ask to live in Harrow Hall!"

"Jennet has made up her mind, and there's nothing I can do to change it," he said, resting his spectacles back on his nose. "I hope you remember that I had nothing to do with it in the nights to follow, m'lass."

"Lethan!" warned Dame Cracklecane, her voice brittle as dry twigs. "I've asked you not to frighten her. I won't put up with it, do you hear?"

"I'm not frightened," Fiona lied, gazing up at the Marl of Harrow. Her wide eyes were puzzled, and she wondered if it was jealousy or concern she had heard in his voice. "I know he didn't mean any harm."

"How generous of you!" he answered, nodding his head in mock deference, but his lip curled in a lopsided grin despite his effort to scowl. "There might be more to you than meets the eye, m'lass."

Fiona did not know what to make of him. He was nothing like the tales she had heard of the Gentry. "I might say the same of you," she murmured, giggling at the consternation in his face. "I look forward to living in Harrow Hall." Lethan nodded curtly as the workmen nudged one another and chortled over their goatskins of wine. Fiona hastily lowered her eyes and gnawed her lip.

Dame Cracklecane mounted her waiting mare. "Fiona, give me your hand," she said, reaching down from the saddle. "You should get out of this fog and into bed. The servants should have hot cider and butternut cakes waiting for us. Does that suit your fancy?"

Fiona nodded, considering the heavy bronze sword in her hand. There was no sense in keeping it, but she did not want to simply throw it back into the mud. Father would probably have kept it as an offering of luck or The Lady. It was best not to offend either of them. She also decided that it made her look sure of herself. I found it and so it belongs to me now! She would not change her mind.

She handed the sword to Dame Cracklecane. "It's mine," she said loudly, digging her toes into the clover. The woman carefully strapped the sword to her saddle. Fiona smiled in satisfaction. "Thank you!"

Dame Cracklecane then pulled the girl into her lap with unexpected ease and strength. "Now, just hold onto her mane, and you'll do fine," she told Fiona. "There, that's the way to do it!—Ready?"

"I think so...."

Scathlings tramped through the fog, and the axles of the wagon groaned as it lurched out of the wood. The deep clover was flecked with drops of gold. Egil led the team of plowing oxen, their humped shoulders straining with the weight of the sagging wagon. Fiona decided that he looked trustworthy—for a southron. She had never met one, but she had heard all the tales about them.

"Jennet?" Lethan cantered up to Dame Cracklecane. "I hope you know what it is you do," he said softly, looking at Fiona. She met his worried gaze and suddenly realized that he was little more than one-and-twenty, although he seemed to be older... Perhaps he hoped to convince himself. He stared coldly at her and then turned his stallion into the gray fog. Fiona watched him dissolve like a ghost.

Her head still hurt. Dame Cracklecane drew it down to her warm breast, smoothing the tangle of auburn hair over the softness of velvet. Fiona smiled drowsily and breathed the wet fog. I wish the orphanage could see me now! The muffled cry of a falcon faded into her yawn, and the stinging brine in the wind could not keep her eyes open. The gentle pace of the mare soon lulled her to sleep.

Two

Fiona walked along the narrow path, leaving the imprint of her slippered feet in the wet moss and loose pebbles. Warm sunlight sifted through the trees like flakes of gold. The gray towers of the hall were tangled in the green wood at her back, the remnant of an ancient preserve, where red deer and wild boar had been hunted each fall by the ennobled ancestors of Harrow. It had once been sprawling, but there was little left except for this sleeping wood. Most of the preserve had been chopped down to build the mills that lined the Cairwell River. The practical music of the huge waterfalls rolled in the wind.

He must own most of Lockhaven. She shook her head. The morning tasted of loam and fresh mint. Why should he have so much wealth? He has more than he can ever use now!

She recognized the gnaw of envy that nestled behind her thoughts, and she dismissed it with an angry toss of her long hair. Mother had told her to bury greed and envy as if they were dripping with plague.

But it was her mother who was taken with the plague and buried in the Haugh. She shivered despite the warmth of the sun. It just wasn't fair!

The path began to darken as she walked on, the branches weaving together over her head, and only scattered patches of gold dappled the roof of damp green leaves and shadows. The creaking and splashing of the tireless waterwheels faded into the wordless sighing of the autumn wind, stirring the leaves like the strings of an ancient harp. There were huge flowers growing along the path, each one a trembling cluster of tiny gold bells, chiming softly in petals of white and saffron. A delicate fragrance of cinnamon wood mingled with that of dry leaves in the air, elusive and poignant.

What were these flowers? She paused, stooping to touch one of the blossoms. Her fingers were stained white with the pollen. She had never seen such flowers.

She wiped her fingers on her cloak, glancing back along the path with uneasy eyes, an inexplicable chill washing over her like the pitiless sea of winter. She had heard of these flowers, but she could not recall when or where, and that was enough to frighten her. There was some old wives' tale... It darted away, and she sighed in frustration.

She went on walking through the wood. It was still hard to believe that she was living at Harrow Hall. She hoped that it was not some awful mistake.

She could not help but laugh at herself. She had wanted to escape the orphanage, and now that she had gotten her wish, she still had misgivings about it.

The path began to wander like the scrawl of a dying man as she went on, leading her deeper into the mossy shadows of the wood, until she stopped with the sudden realization that she was lost.

Now what do I do? She turned, looking back in vain for the towers of Harrow Hall. I don't want them to come looking for me as if I were some little girl. Dear Lady, I couldn't bear that!

She gently bit down on her lip in thought. The moss of the path had turned into fallen leaves, so that no imprint of her feet remained to mark her way, and the thick roof of the wood blocked out the sun. She could no longer hear the sound of the waterwheels.

There was no need to be afraid, she told herself. But as the shadows of the wood began to deepen, she glanced about with eyes that flickered like moths' wings. I didn't think I was that far from the hall.

The abrupt noise of rustling leaves made her jump, and she glimpsed the tall antlers of a stag as it leaped through the underbrush, blood running from its flank. She listened for hunting horns, but none called after it, and she had the sense of witnessing something ancient yet familiar.

She took several steps after it, and the sun glinted on bronze through the wet branches, touching the leaves with dim smudges of gold.

It might be an old hunting lodge, she told herself, but the uneasiness she had felt on the path brushed her skin with plumes of ice. She ignored it. I certainly can't stay here all day!

The spoor of the wounded stag led into the wood, toward the glint of bronze in the dark branches, and she followed it with mounting curiosity. The shadows seemed to pluck at her cloak, but the vague fears that gathered like spiderwebs were shrugged away with an impatient toss of her head. She would not let herself turn back now that she had started, even when the gentle underbrush turned into brambles and nettles. She was too stubborn to admit that she might be wrong, especially after coming this far, and she merely became more determined with each new scratch.

It can't be that far away! She grimaced as she yanked her tangled hair away from thick branches. I just hope that it's worth all this nuisance!

The wood opened into a wide glade of hollyhock with her next step, and she caught her breath at the ruins that loomed before her in solemn stillness, overgrown with black ivy and nettles. There was nothing but a crumbling tower, its bronze crown mottled with verdigris, and huge gates of oak and iron stained dark red with rust. Yet there was an air of ageless, slumbering strength about the ruins that touched Fiona. She entered the glade wearing silence like a shawl.

Who could have lived here? She slowly walked up to the massive gates. They must have lived long ago, when the world was still made of legends.

Fiona thought of the mills and workhouses that clogged Lockhaven. Their walls were made of dreary red brick, and the roofs of gray slate. She angrily jabbed her hands into her pockets. There was certainly no place in the world that she knew for legends.

She looked up at the immense pillars that supported the gates. How tall they seemed now that she stood beneath them! She gingerly touched one of the pillars through its dripping shroud of ivy. It had been carved with the visages of kings, their crowns woven with alder leaves, but their features had been blurred by the grinding of the seasons. Ivy had crawled into the cracks, burrowing with countless tendrils until the stone was riddled like an old log. Chunks of the pillar were already strewn in the hollyhock.

Soon there'll be nothing left. She let the dank mat of ivy fall back into place, wondering if anyone else would care that this was all going to ruin. She doubted it. Folk were more interested in the present. And perhaps that was all for the best. Her own father had thought so.

She tapped her fingers over the crumbling iron doors of the gates, and rust flaked off like the withered leaves that whispered to themselves in the wind. Ivy trailed out of the shapeless lock. It seemed impossible that these gates could ever be opened, even with gunpowder and battering ram.

And then she snatched her fingers away from the rusting doors, for her idle tapping had been answered from within the tower. She held her breath as something beat upon the other side of the gates, fumbling with the lock. But nothing could be alive in there—!

Huge cracks slithered through the doors, and the hinges groaned under pounding blows. Fiona clutched for the goad in her pocket. She was unable to move, although her legs shook like reeds. The gates lurched open before her, and something reached out from the darkness behind them. She bit into her lip without feeling it.

"I've been waiting for you, Fiona..." And at last she turned to flee, even as bony fingers clamped about her wrist. "I've been waiting the longest time, my sweetling...." Fear smothered her as she was dragged inside the gates... only to sit up in bed, sobbing for breath, her bedclothes soaked with sweat.

"It was a dream." She trembled, brushing the lank hair from her eyes with darting fingers. "That's all it was, only a dream."

The moonlight was cold and white as frost upon the gray stone of the floor. It poured in through large windows, and embers smoldered on the hearth. The walls were polished oak panels, and the black door was set with twining vines of wan gold. There was a clay mug and a pitcher of water placed on the table by her bed. She reached for the pitcher, stopping as she saw the ornate crest graven in the dull pewter. What was she doing in this strange room?

"I'm in Harrow Hall," she remembered. Dame Cracklecane had tucked her into bed, leaving the hot cider and butternut cakes for another night. She rubbed her eyes and hoped that this was not the dream. It was nothing like her simple room at Balestone House.

She drank some water, wiping her mouth on the corner of the brocaded sheet. The lingering fears of her dream made it impossible to go back to sleep. She got out of bed, pulling one of the blankets about her fine linen bedclothes, and went to the hearth.

There was an oil painting of three children placed over the mantel, and she recognized one of them as Lethan.

He was between another boy and an older girl, all three standing in dark green ferns. The boys were clad in gold and russet, while the girl wore royal blue, and all were swathed in yellow cloaks. The resemblance joined them as family. Fiona saw an eloquence in the brash features of the girl that touched her, and she had an intuition that the girl had painted this portrait. It was both subdued and impetuous with childhood.

Her feet were cold despite the coals on the hearth, and she reached for her slippers, only to catch her breath as she touched them.

The red velvet of the slippers was thick with clumps of moss and clinging to one was a crushed flower like tiny gold bells, trembling in broken petals of white and saffron. The flower stained her fingers white with pollen, and the air was fragrant with cinnamon wood.

Fiona felt her heart pounding as if it would burst, and she dropped the slippers to the floor with a horrified scream that echoed through the room.

"My dear—!"

"Do something, Gwyn!"

She struggled against the strong hands that grasped her flailing arms and sat her down upon the bed, and she did not gain control of herself until she heard the comforting voice of Dame Cracklecane. She bit down into her lip, letting the pain burn away her fear like a cauterizing iron.

"Fiona, stop it!" Dame Cracklecane snapped, wiping the blood from her mouth. "Do you want to give yourself an ugly scar?"

Fiona gingerly felt her swollen lip. "What's happening to me?" she pleaded, huddling under the heavy blankets. "I'm so cold!"

The room slowly filled with firelight. Lethan stood at the hearth, his bedclothes grimy with ash. "Well?" he asked Dame Cracklecane. "I warned you that this could happen, but you wouldn't hear of it." He picked the dead flower off the floor and tossed it into the fire. "You might at least have warned the child."

"I never dreamed that it would start so soon," retorted Dame Cracklecane. "You seem quite learned in the lore of the Mark."

"Lore has always been the province of my family," said the Marl. He stirred the coals with an iron poker, steeping his lean face in shadows. The faces in the painting looked down at him in disturbing innocence. "You should understand my interest in the Mark."

"I do, Lethan."

When did they come into the room? Fiona thought numbly but could not remember. How long had she been screaming into the darkness of the room?

Dame Cracklecane smiled tenderly at Fiona. "I hoped to wait until morning, but perhaps it is best to tell you now," she said. "I'll have the servants fetch some mulled cider."

"Jennet, not here."

Dame Cracklecane looked at the girl in the painting. "I understand," she said gently. "We'll talk in the scholary if you wish."

"Thank you," he said, haunted by the stillness of the room. "I'll go and stir up the hearth." He left for the scholary, rubbing the nape of his neck.

Fiona slowly put on the woolen robe offered her by Dame Cracklecane. She still felt cold, but she left her feet bare rather than touch her slippers. "What's wrong with me?" she moaned, wiping her clammy brow. "I'm going to be ill." Dame Cracklecane helped her stand. "I feel dizzy now."

"I know how confused you must be, my dear." The woman clasped her hand and led her into the oaken hall. "There is no excuse for my negligence. I recall what it was like for me at thirteen. I should have given you some warning."

"You had bad dreams?"

"Oh, terrible dreams!" She laughed, but she could not disguise the fears that lingered from her childhood. "I put away all dreams long ago." Fiona glanced at her, taking in the weary lines about her eyes, the disheveled mass of black hair like a bird's nest. "I don't want you to be afraid of your heritage, Fiona."

Fiona was not certain that she wanted to learn of that heritage. She could feel her stomach churning, and her legs were like jelly. "I'm not afraid," she said, pulling her hand away from the woman.

The hall grew warmer as rich hearthlight shone through the arch of black oak and hammered gold that opened upon the scholary. "Here we are," said Dame Cracklecane. "Do watch your footing, my dear."

The room was large, its dark oaken rafters bearded with dry herbs, its gray floor strewn with sweet rushes. Curls of flame rose lazily from the coals on the long hearth, and two iron pokers with carved oak handles leaned in an ornate stand of polished brass. The diamond panes of the windows glinted with frost.

The table of gleaming cedar was set with an astrolabe of bronze, three goblets of fine crystal, and an antique ewer of white gold that brimmed with wine. The racks of the enormous table were filled with scrolls and hornbooks. An oak writing board jutted from its drawer in the table, where the nib of a gold-tipped quill burned in the firelight.

Fiona saw only the magnificent tapestry that covered an entire wall in lush, eloquent hues, depicting The Lady in the Witchwood.

She stood beneath the branches of an oak, Her slim hand set on its gnarled bole, the wind stirring Her robe of green leaves and wet silver spiderwebs. Her dark chestnut tresses were woven into the branches of the oak, and Her unshod feet were rooted in the damp earth, mantled in sweet clover. Her face was made of pale white flowers speckled with blood, and Her eyes were the green of ancient moss, swirling with motes of vivid gold. The slow, quiet strength of earth, water and wood was immanent in Her unmoving form, and the dawn crowned Her with glory.

Fiona realized how old the tapestry must be, and caught her breath, for it could not have been woven save in the dawn of the world, when The Lady still walked the newborn meadows and hills She had shaped from the cold, dead earth of another world. It seemed more real than the room which it dominated with power and beauty.

Lethan chuckled at the hearth, where three chairs stood before the drowsy coals. "It can draw you into its depths if you watch it long enough," he said, tossing dried herbs into the fire. "The hours you spend before it seem to pass in one eager heartbeat."

Fiona turned her eyes from the shimmering tapestry with effort. "Where did you ever find this treasure?" she asked in quiet wonder. "It's so—" She raised her hands in wordless defeat.

"You speak more truly than you can know." Dame Cracklecane smiled. "It is indeed one of the forgotten treasures of Therrilyn."

Fiona sat down in one of the chairs, wriggling her toes over the hearth. "Therrilyn?" she said. "That's just an old legend, isn't it?"

Dame Cracklecane looked at Lethan. "Well, do you hear that?" she demanded angrily. "Do you hear what she has been taught in that orphanage? There is no place in letters and figures for the truth of legends!" She turned to Fiona. "I shall tell you of Therrilyn."

The room was still. Dame Cracklecane began to speak in the flowing cadence of an oracle, her voice like the tolling of distant bells at the edge of sleep.

"In the beginning was The Lady. The seas were of blood and the earth made of ash, for Her children had sought power and dominion over the world She had birthed, only to destroy both their world and themselves in blackest madness. And so The Lady wept, Her hot tears falling to the earth, and where they fell were healed the scars of war and destruction. And so the earth was imbued with new life, still bound in stone, silence and slumber, yet stirring with the vast power of The Lady.

"Now The Lady spilled the blood of Her womanhood across the waiting earth, awakening the life in river and wood, moor and meadow, valley and mountain: and the milk of Her breasts nurtured the earth: and the daughters of Her womb peopled the earth. And this pleased The Lady.

"Now The Lady bore twin sons, and gave them dominion of the sun and the moon, and named them Haldir and Holdir. But each desired to possess Her Love for himself alone, and they fought for an age, striking the stars like sparks from their swords, until The Lady parted them forever between the gates of dusk and dawn. But the stars that fell from their swords kindled strife in those who found them, and so the shadow of war entered into the world once more.

"Yet there was also wonder in the world, for the shadow was dim, and the many daughters of The Lady wielded the Fire that banishes darkness. The noblest of them was Ygerna, who took to herself many kings from the warriors who served her, and with lore and beauty founded the realm of Therrilyn. In the countless centuries of her reign the People of the Stone were buried in Nethernesse, and the People of the Root bound under the Witchwood. And over all the land was the peace of The Lady.

"Yet the shadow remained, for there were strongholds in the deep places of the earth that had never been cleansed by the tears of The Lady. And those who served in the House of Holdir delved in the earth, seeking the power that slumbered in those strongholds of the World-Before-the-World, for they dreamed of crushing the House of Haldir. And so the ancient evil was loosed upon the world, and so was born the realm of Witcherie.

"There was war, and there was burning, and there was an endless shedding of blood, until both realms became one, and both realms perished from the earth."

The hearth crackled with embers and aromatic herbs, but the room felt cold to Fiona. "What happened after that?" she asked, remembering the folk tales of gaunts and skin-walkers and witchwives that made up her vague notion of the past.

"Ygerna fell in battle, and with her fell also the House of Holdir," said the woman. "She was buried in the old tomb of Mymmorë." The bed of hot embers burst loudly at her feet. "There she shall sleep until the hour of her awakening, as it was prophesied by the last oracles of The Lady—but we shall speak of that another time, my dear. Now you must learn what followed the ruin of Therrilyn."

"What was that?"

"There were centuries of fear and war, truly called the Age of the Axe," said Dame Cracklecane. "You've surely heard of that! Tribe after tribe of southrons came plundering out of the Plains of Har. Maelings, then Scathlings, and even in our own time the horse-tails, who so grandly call themselves the People of the Stallion Banner. There were famines, which led to scores of witch trials ending in the fire-pit or upon the gibbet." She gazed moodily into the fire. "Kelgardh was the only bastion of lore and wisdom that remained, and those of our kindred who had survived led the world to believe that it was merely an enormous scholary, which it became over the years." She shook her head. "Such was the foundation of the Mark."

The fire deepened the anger in her eyes. "We must hide ourselves from a world that no longer believes in us, nor in The Lady."

"You fail to mention the abbeys of Haldir," Lethan said curtly. "The harpists and goodwives have preserved much that might have been lost, even if our ancestors were little more than barbarians from the hills of Mael."

"This is so, but their knowledge was not rooted in the worship of The Lady," said Dame Cracklecane. "Mystery is the root of life, and without it, your knowledge grows barren."

She rose to stand before the crackling hearth. "Do you now begin to understand your heritage?" she asked Fiona. "It is the power that vanquished the darkness: it is the Fire of The Lady."

Dame Cracklecane slowly raised her hands as a nimbus of silver fire gathered like dew about her rigid form, shimmering over her flesh without harm, until she was transfigured into a living star. The radiance was most blinding at her brow and her hands, but there was no heat—the sweet rushes underfoot did not burn. The air was redolent of turned loam and early thaw and lightning-scorched stone. There were sparks of hot gold in her hair.

"Do you see?" She laughed, and her voice was a harp of moonlight and water, filling the room with delight. "This is your heritage!"

"No," whispered Fiona. She clutched at the arms of her chair, fingers white upon the carved black oak. "It can't be true!"

Dame Cracklecane held out her hands, anointed with the rich, earthen smells of damp summer. "You mustn't be afraid of this precious gift," she said gently. "It is yours."

"No, it's not true!" insisted Fiona. She knew better than to believe in such things. Yet the pervading smells of meadow and soil invoked memories of childhood, when she lived with her family on the farm, and she felt a sudden yearning to believe Dame Cracklecane. "It can't be true."

"It is true," murmured Dame Cracklecane. "You can feel it awakening within your heart. Come. You need only take my hand to accept the gift of The Lady."

Fiona slowly reached out and took her hand. The moment that she touched the silver fire her heart seemed to burst in embers and ice. Tendrils of bittersweet pain twined through her breast, flowering into a blossom of black flame, and then the pain awakened into such consuming warmth that she closed her eyes and bit deeply into her lip.

She tasted blood as she opened her eyes, gaping down at the beads of silver fire that trembled in her hands like cold moonlight. It guttered out even as she watched, but beneath the fragile beauty she could sense the wellsprings of immense power that flowed through her, unknown and primordial as the blood of the earth.

She sagged in the oaken chair as the feeling of strength suddenly drained from her limbs, leaving her weak as a newborn colt, her white face glistening with sweat. Dame Cracklecane helped her to sit up.

"What happened to me?" breathed Fiona, gulping down the goblet of wine proffered by Lethan. "I didn't think it would be like that." She shook her head. "I feel so tired!"

"I know, but it will pass." Dame Cracklecane stretched her arms with a loud creaking of bones. The firelight carved lines of age in her weary face. "It is not easy to wield or rein the Fire. I'll teach you all that you must know, for it is perilous." She gazed up at the tapestry. "Yet what gift of beauty is not perilous? You shouldn't look so worried, my dear."

"What of my dreams?"

"The least of hunting fires will draw moths," said Dame Cracklecane. "The fire of sorcery tends to draw other things out of the night."

"What other things?"

"Dead leaves, shadows, bones, or even torrents of fiery gold. There is no end to the things that manifest themselves in the light of the Fire." She plucked a warm coal from the hearth and dropped it into her goblet of wine. "These things are spun out of our dreams." The tang of mulled wine filled the room. "Some are frail and beautiful, while some are dark and fearsome. So it is with our dreams. It would be better for you to ignore them."

Fiona leaned forward in her chair. "Why is that?" she asked, fearing that the woman had smoothed over something too troubling in her effort to espouse the Mark. "What happens in our dreams?"

Dame Cracklecane put one hand firmly upon the astrolabe of gleaming bronze. "There are secrets that can be caught by the minds of men, just as the fixed stars are caught by this cunning device, but there are other secrets that can never be gutted and shorn of their mystery, my dear."

"You don't know—?"

"It has nothing to do with knowledge," Dame Cracklecane said coldly. She held the astrolabe as if longing to crumple it into shapeless ruin. "Such things are of the mysteries." Lethan shook his head but said nothing. "I will see that you sleep without dreams."

Fiona sipped at the dregs of her wine. "What about the orphanage?" she asked, yawning despite herself at the mention of sleep. "I won't go back to Balestone House!"

"You needn't worry about the orphanage," Lethan assured her, rising from his chair. "I'll have the parchment scribed and sealed according to the Law." Dame Cracklecane wrinkled her nose. "I hope that you have no objection to becoming the ward of Harrow Hall?"

"What does that mean?" Fiona stood up and glowered at him with suspicion. "I won't live here if it means fetching your tea and scrubbing the floors! I had enough of that in the orphanage!"

"It means nothing of the sort, m'lass," Lethan replied with mild irritation. "Now, why don't you just run along to your bed?" Fiona set down her goblet of wine and turned to leave the scholary. "Hold," he said kindly. "I'll show you to your room."

"I can find my own way back," she said, her voice quiet but petulant. She hurried down the hall, one hand following the wall of carved ivy and cracklecane until she came to her room. Moonlight shone through frosted windows as she opened the door. She looked up at the painting over the hearth and climbed into bed.

I hope that this isn't some awful mistake. She punched the down pillows into comfortable shape and burrowed under the heavy blankets. The hearth crackled sleepily with crumbling embers. She giggled to herself. It was certainly better than living at Balestone House.

Gwyneth brooded over the hearth, stirring the coals and ashes with an iron poker, ignoring the sparks that singed her fine linen bedclothes. There was so much depending upon one child!

"Dame Cracklecane." She frowned, looking down into the coals for answers that eluded her. What had made her choose that name? It only reminded her of Weland.

"Ah, Weland..."

She jabbed at the coals, raising ashes and sparks. The

pity! She sighed angrily, watching as the coals settled into smoldering laziness. He could have had so much, but he fell prey to his fears and he lost himself. He lost all that was precious to him.

The coals burned red as the blood that had splashed the walls when she found Maeve. The woman had been sprawled upon the floor of the cottage, still clutching the broken form of her newborn daughter. Weland had stood numbly at the window, his hands dripping with more blood, watching as the scarlies blotted out the gaping moon. The cold realization of what he had done would not possess him until morning, and months would pass before he could be entrusted with his own life. There was nothing more to be done, and he had drifted away like so much wreckage, settling in the villages of the Scathe.

Gwyneth looked up at the tapestry. She chose to recall earlier days, when he had been one of her companions upon the journey to Pel Lendwrei. Weland had found the tapestry when they descended into the depths of the ruined city, and hordes of gaunts fell upon them with axes of flint, led by one clad in rotting finery who wielded one of the Four Stones. It had taken three nights to defeat them, and when it was done, not one of the foul creatures lived. Yet that had been the start of his fear, and it had grown worse, until at last he sought denial in his marriage to Maeve.

"Ah, Maeve..."

What had become of them all?

She set the poker to one side and turned to the hearth. The silver fire gathered about her, an unbroken veil of weary glow and mist. She slowly reached down and touched the warm ashes on the hearth. The dying embers refused to blaze up in flame, and if there was an omen in it, she recognized it for an unwanted truth.

The gift was fading. She rose to her feet, leaving the coals encrusted with hoarfrost, as the nimbus of silver fire dissolved into cold mist. Fiona must be the one to take her place in the Mark.

The darkness steeped the room in gloomy shadow, and she lit a candle with one of the awkward, sputtering matches that had begun to replace tinder and flint. The soft yellow glow of the candle comforted her. She walked to the table and sat down to ponder the past. The mocking astrolabe gleamed with certainty and precision. There were no such tools to measure and predict the course of her life. It was so unlike her to desire such things that she wondered if her fears were really premonitions.

I worry far too much. She carefully rubbed the nape of her neck, wincing as she felt the bones crack. Dear Lady! I feel so old tonight!

Gwyneth watched the hot wax melting like years down the side of the solitary candle, unable to dispel the encroaching gloom. Her power was fading like the dried rushes under her feet. What could she call her own after devoting her life to The Lady? She had no family, and would never have one, for all the aching in her heart. She had nothing but her life in the Mark.

The candle spilled her shadow upon the rich tapestry in flickering light. She looked up with longing and loss at the beautiful face of flowers, calm beneath the trembling of her shadow, and murmured the prayers of her childhood. She would never deny The Lady.

Her sighing prayers faltered as she remembered all that had been done for the sake of The Lady. There had been lies, and worse than lies, leading her to that night in the lonely heather of the Haugh. She loathed what had been done, but it was necessary—or so said Helskarth. Yet he was right, she admitted to herself. Why dwell upon her qualms? It was done for the greatest good....Gwyneth only hoped that she would never have to tell Fiona. It pained her that she must lie to the girl, but it was necessary to gain her trust. —And where was the sense in *that* witless notion?

Gwyneth slowly kneaded the small of her back. There was so much to be done, and so little time in which to do it! She had begun to fray like so much shoddy cloth from the mills of Lockhaven.

"Gwyn?" said Lethan. He was swathed in a patched cloak and wore muddy boots. "I've been around back," he explained, striding into the room. Bits of leaves clung to his tousled hair, which he brushed back. "I heard something moving about in the woods."

"You shouldn't do that, especially in the middle of the night," Gwyneth said, fear bobbing in her throat. But it was useless to chide him. "What was it?"

"Probably a wild boar snuffling for roots and nuts," he said, drawing the flintlock pistol from his cloak and setting it on the table. "My fears might be foolish, but that child puts me in mind of Elspeth." His face was grim in the yellow glow of the candle, which flickered in his spectacles like a ghost. "I won't go through that horror again."

"You won't have to, my dear." Gwyneth refused to look at the ugly pistol as she gently touched his cheek. "Elspeth is not beyond help," she assured him, letting her hand fall to his breast. "Fiona is our hope, for the gift burns within her like the very stars. There were few to match her power even in the days of Therrilyn." She smiled quietly. "Please don't worry, Lethan."

"She'll be my responsibility under the Law." His voice was firm. "I'm hoping to help my sister, but not if it means leaving another in her place, Gwyn." He clasped the fingers that lay gently upon his breast. "You must surely understand my feelings—?"

"Yes, of course," she said quickly, filling the silence between them. "You needn't worry about Fiona. I'll see that she's not hurt." His hand was still clasping hers. "This won't go on much longer, my dear."

"Well, that's a blessing," he said bluntly. "I haven't liked having to lie to my family, even if it is for their own peace of mind." He felt the weight of ancestral presence in the shadows of the room. "I would have gotten a birching for such babble if my father ever heard it. —But he is ten years dead now. I am the Marl." Lethan shook his head. "I merely hope to follow in his path. That is, if my feet are not too small to fill his boots." He laughed uneasily. "We'll let a cobbler be the judge of that! I've other matters concerning me these days. I'll have to have some magistrate's scribe prepare the decree of wardship for the girl, but that should be simple enough...." He seemed more comfortable speaking of the Law. "What are you smiling at, Jennet?"

"You needn't be so earnest," she said tenderly, an ache in her throat. What must it have been like, growing up in the memory of a man such as Helmeric? "But you were always like that, even as a little boy, so plainly a scholar. Your father always believed that you should be the next Marl."

He softly kissed her brow. "Elsie would have been the Marl," he said, brushing the sweet strands of black hair from her face. "I wanted nothing more than the life of a scholar in Bridging Hall. But there are too many threads in life for one to discern its pattern. I fear it's all that one can do to choose even a handful for the loom." Lethan gently pulled her closer to him. The fragrance of her hair swirled in his senses with every breath. "You shouldn't be walking about in your bedclothes."

"I must attend to Fiona," she said, reluctantly drawing away from his warm embrace, but lingering at the touch of his hand. "I'll be with you soon, my dearest."

He laughed ruefully as the one candle guttered out with

a sigh. "I'll be waiting," he murmured, and walked down the dark hall. Gwyneth watched in silence, the ache catching in her throat.

She had never felt that gentle ache until the last days of summer, when he appeared at her door in the village of Dyrning. He had been little more than five when she had seen him last, before the death of Maeve. Now he was a young man, his heart unpoisoned and eager to learn of the Mark. So she had taken him into her home, wary at first, amused by his earnest manner, and found herself falling in love with him.

She had returned with him in autumn, entering the house from which she had been driven years ago by Helmeric. It was uncomfortable at first, but she had been spared the childish humiliation of hiding from his family. He now lived alone in Harrow Hall. Pendric, his younger brother, was tramping his way down country roads with his harp. Merúshe, his mother, was the Abbess of Lockhaven. The huge house had been cleared of all but the most necessary servants. But nothing could clear it of the memories that lingered in every room. She endured these like wounds.

She walked down the long hall to the room that had been given to Fiona. The door opened at her touch, and she entered with the stealth of the moonlight that fell like milk on the floor. Fiona was almost lost in the blankets that covered the oaken bed.

The windows shivered. Gwyneth saw that dead leaves were beating against the diamond panes like huge moths, black with runes of web and soot. She swallowed the fear that lumped in her throat. The girl in the painting looked down at her with troubled eyes. She turned gracefully to Fiona.

Here was the daughter she had never been granted by The Lady. She raised her arms, summoning up the power that still burned within her, ignoring the painful throb of her heart.

A swirling cloud of silver fire slowly gathered between her hands, burning away the shadows that clung to Fiona. Her freckled face was vulnerable in the shimmering of the silver fire. The dead leaves beat against the windows with mounting fury. Gwyneth held her breath, but the pale windows did not shatter. She breathed gratefully, her heart pounding angrily within her breast. Embers burst loudly on the hearth as she lowered her hands to anoint Fiona.

"Dream no more this night," Gwyneth whispered, raising her hands and stepping away from the bed. Fiona murmured in her sleep, but the trembling nimbus of silver fire upon her brow shielded her from all dreams. It would serve until the wards had been set within her mind. Gwyneth hoped that the girl would be equal to the tasks that awaited her. But that must be the judgment of The Lady.

A single leaf clung to the window, its withered shadow limned upon the floor by the leering moon. Gwyneth took care not to step on it as she left the room.

Three

FIONA FELT HER THROAT GROWING taut as the coach rattled into the courtyard of Balestone House, a flurry of red leaves in its wake. She could smell the familiar porridge, and she wrinkled her nose, remembering how often she had struggled to force it down without honey or butter. It had tasted of the dishwater that was used to scrub the pots, and the memory was enough to make her feel ill.

How did I manage to endure that? She frowned, watching the morning sun flash in raucous gold from the windows of the kitchen. The food was the least of it.

"I'll speak to the headmistress," Dame Cracklecane said as the coach halted before the main house, looming in ivy and weathered gray stone above the courtyard. "You go and fetch your things."

Fiona did not really want to go back in, not even for her few belongings. She smoothed the folds of her dark green kirtle, tracing the pale gold of its twining vines and new leaves with one finger. Now she truly felt ill.

She stepped from the coach, her hair stirring in dozens of thin braids over her shoulders, and slowly gazed about the courtyard. The cobblestones were bearded with thistles, and the long hedges of rowan needed pruning. Small children were gathered beneath an oak, playing Skip-the-Stone. The lowest branches of the oak reached down to scratch the gray slate of the kitchen roof. The tartness of apples mingled with brine in the damp breeze, and she heard the ocean pounding the foot of the cliffs, bitter as the bile rising in her throat. She swallowed and walked beside Dame Cracklecane.

"Now, this shouldn't take very long," she said, smiling with reassurance at Fiona. "Do hurry back as soon as you are done, my dear."

"Yes," said Fiona. She looked up at the bright red and yellow lion painted on the black door, its fierce jaws gaping at them. "There's very little for me here."

Dame Cracklecane nodded slightly and rang the iron bell that was clasped in the paws of the lion. Red flakes of rust drifted to her feet. The door was opened by a woman clad in the folded red mantle and white kirtle of the goodwives. The wealstone gleaming on her breast was made of gold. She held a birch rod in one hand, and her face grew pinched with anger when she saw Fiona.

"Where have you been?" she demanded, switching the cold air with the birch rod. Wisps of brown hair trailed from the tidy bun she wore clasped with two wooden pegs. "The wagon for the workhouse left before dawn!"

Dame Cracklecane drew herself up disdainfully, looking down at the goodwife. "Fiona, who is this woman?" she asked without warmth. "I should like to know her name."

"Goody Gulde," muttered Fiona, looking at the birch rod and remembering how often it had bloodied her aching fingers until she could not close them. "She teaches things."

Dame Cracklecane heard the bitterness in those muttered words and said, "Goody Gulde, is it? I can imagine what you teach. Well, go and fetch the headmistress!"

"Who are you?" said Goody Gulde. Her pale eyes glinted icily in the sun. "What business do you have with Balestone House?"

"Fiona will be leaving with me." Dame Cracklecane held up a thick scroll of parchment that bore the red seal of the Law. "Now, will you fetch the headmistress at once?"

"What's this nonsense?" The goodwife put on spectacles to read the parchment with care, tucking the birch rod under one arm. "I can't understand who would be foolish enough to take in this brat." She shook her head. "I have no dispute with the Law. Good riddance to her!"

Dame Cracklecane smiled with satisfaction, taking back the scroll with an amused wink to Fiona. "You'll allow the child to collect her things?"

"Let her do just as she pleases." Goody Gulde spoke as sourly as vinegar. "What else has she ever done since coming here, the numbwit?"

Fiona swallowed bile. *I loathe her so!* She watched as the woman turned and walked down the hall, clasping the birch rod with bony knuckles. *I don't ever want to see her again! Dear Lady, let her be struck dead on the spot!*

"Well," murmured Dame Cracklecane. Her eyes shone with anger, and she wiped her fingers on her cloak. "I'll wait for you here, but don't take too long, my dear."

"I won't."

Fiona walked down the hall, one hand deep in the pocket of her warm green cloak, clutching the smooth cattle goad for strength. The morning light was dim with dust, and she felt as if her heart had frozen, reliving the months she had spent enduring this place. Her steps echoed like taunts.

She had worn her fingers raw scrubbing the floors of these halls. How many times had she been punished for her defiance of the rules?

She went up the narrow stairs, wincing as the old steps creaked beneath her feet, which were now shod in soft doeskin rather than the wooden shoes that one of the workhouses made for Balestone House. She clung to the polished brass railing to keep from stumbling over the familiar steps she had taken countless times.

The head of the stairs opened upon an oak and slate hall of doors painted bright yellow. Fiona counted them off until she came to her room. There was little light, and she folded the wooden shutters back. Sunlight poured through the window into the cramped room.

There was not much to take with her, but she gathered up some patched farm clothes, her stout wading boots, her floppy cap of rabbit fur, and her long brown scarf. What else? She sat down on the straw pallet of her bed. It was difficult to believe that so little had marked her presence in this silent room. The rest belonged to the orphanage.

She took one of the hornbooks from its oaken peg on the wall, remembering how many times she had been birched for not reciting her letters, ashamed to admit that she did not know them.

What is so important about that? She angrily threw the hornbook on the floor. Father never learned how to read, and it never troubled him! What if children half my age do know their letters? I wager none of them ever hunted hares with a sling, or helped fight off hungry wolves with firebrands, or learned to shoot a musket!

She flopped back on the bed, gazing up at the cracks in the ceiling, and clasped the thin pillow behind her head. It galled her that she could not read, but she refused to admit that, even to herself. Goody Gulde wanted her to read, which made her more determined not to learn, even when her fingers were birched almost to the bone. She was too stubborn to let herself back away from her defiant stance once she had taken it, no matter how foolish it was, choosing to be proud of her defiance. Or was it merely ignorance?

She sighed in confusion. The faint droning of students at morning recitations rose through the floor. Those who had proven unwilling to learn were now busy in the workhouses of Lockhaven. She would have been laboring with them if not for Dame Cracklecane.

She thought of the gift of the Fire. She still did not know

whether to believe in it, despite all she had been shown by Dame Cracklecane. It troubled her to think of possessing such power, for she did not believe in gifts. One had to pay some price for all things.

The room smelled of dried herbs and dust. She breathed in the familiar scent and wondered what her life would be like in Harrow Hall. Father would have warned her against taking up with the Gentry. But surely it would be better than living another day in Balestone House!

Perhaps her new surroundings would be too uncomfortably rich for the likes of a farm girl. No! She was just as good as any coddled child of the Gentry!

"Fiona?"

"Who is it?"

Deirdre opened the door. She wore the same homespun as the other children, and her amber hair was coiled at the nape of her neck in a peasant's knot, but her features were those of the Gentry. Hard work had given warmth to what might have been cold beauty, and the crooked tooth that she revealed as she smiled made her more appealing.

"I was fetching tea for the headmistress." She glanced nervously about the drab room. "Are you really going to live at Harrow Hall?"

Fiona nodded uncomfortably, clasping the cattle goad in her pocket. "Why do you ask?" she said, her eyes narrow with suspicion.

Deirdre carefully shut the door behind her at the sound of footsteps in the hall. "I'm not supposed to be here," she explained with an awkward smile. "I just wanted to wish you good fortune." The footsteps dwindled, and she gave an angry sigh of relief. "I'm glad that someone is getting away from this heartless place. You certainly deserve it more than the rest of us. What have we done but meekly obey the rules?"

Fiona looked at her with astonishment. "What's gotten

into you?" she asked, glimpsing the bitterness in those dark gray eyes. "I've never heard anything like that from you!" She suddenly felt embarrassed. "I thought that you liked it here."

"I was the dutiful girl with the sweet smile." Deirdre laughed too loudly in mockery. "I go on smiling until my jaw throbs with it," she added, turning to the window. Her face seemed pale and lost. "I can't bear any more of this without choking on it!"

She lowered her eyes, unable to stop the tears that ran down her cheeks. "It really isn't fair," she said, her voice shaking with each word. "Why should you be the one with all the courage? I'll never be able to stand up to them like you do, Fiona." She desperately wiped away her tears. "I don't know how to be strong. It was always enough to be pretty for everyone. Pretty!"

"What's wrong with that?"

"They all love a goosy girl called Deirdre. I wouldn't know who she is, because all we've got in common is the same name." She turned from the window. "I sometimes believe it would be much easier to turn into that other Deirdre. I can be even more simpering and witless. I've been pretending to be her all of my life." Her laughter was harsh. "Who would ever want to know just me, Deirdre?"

The orphanage bells rang out the hour, lingering in the closed room. "I could never do that," Fiona said, looking at the floor. "How could you?"

"I lacked your courage," Deirdre said, wavering between shame and accusation. "I didn't know what else to do! Does that make me a coward?"

Fiona felt more uncomfortable than ever, and she had no inkling of what to say to the troubled girl. "Why should you tell all of this to me?" she asked, fumbling with one of her braids. "We were never friends."

"I know." Deirdre lowered her head. "I don't blame you for it," she said softly. "Why would someone like you bother with someone like me? You wouldn't know what it's like to be lonely and hurt."

This was too much to believe. "You can't be jealous of *me!*" exclaimed Fiona. "The others always followed you around like bees after honey! So did the warders! I was always in trouble—and that wasn't courage! I was just stubborn." She gave an uneasy laugh. "I was jealous of *you,* Deirdre." The older girl looked up in disbelief. "I didn't enjoy scrubbing the floors, especially with birched fingers! I wanted to be like you, and have lots of friends, and be so—pretty!" The words caught in her throat. "We didn't know each other very well," she sighed. "We might have been friends."

Deirdre sat down beside her on the bed. "Do you really mean that we *could* be friends?" she said eagerly, laughing in delight. "I'd like that, even if you are leaving this awful house." She abruptly spat on the floor, startling Fiona. "I heard them talking about you in the lower hall. Goody Gulde said that you were being rewarded for insolence, and that you should be sent to the mills."

"She would say that, the heartless sow." Fiona clasped the goad in her pocket. "I never want to see her again. —But let's not talk about her." She smiled hesitantly. "Perhaps you could visit me at Harrow Hall?"

"I don't think they would allow it," said Deirdre. Her soft voice had turned bitter with resignation. "Someone will always try to run our lives for us, deciding what's best for us, because we're not old enough to do that for ourselves! I loathe that! What we want doesn't matter, not to them! And they want you to be *grateful* for it!" She struggled to catch her breath. "And you *have* to be grateful! They want to *see* it! And you do what they want. You just do."

The silence was bare and raw. Deirdre folded her hands in her lap. Fiona stood up, gathering her few things into an awkward bundle. "I have to go now," she muttered, desperate to leave the cramped room. "You'll come and visit. You have to, or I'll come here to visit. You'll see!"

"They wouldn't like that."

Fiona could feel the power stirring within her, and she smiled thinly. "I don't care if they like it or not, because I'm going to do just as I please," she said, opening the oak door as if she longed to rip it from its brass hinges. "I've had my fill of doing what others want!" The yellow sunlight sifted about her, pale as dry straw. "You just have to stand up for yourself, Deirdre."

Deirdre laughed weakly and shook her head. "They'll be pleased to be rid of you," she said wistfully. "I might come calling after all." But her fingers were knotted tightly in her lap.

"I'll be waiting for you," Fiona said, walking into the stillness of the hall with a dim rustling of her kirtle. She smoothed the distracting folds. The stillness went numb.

She turned and hurried to the stairs, clutching her few belongings to her breast. Dame Cracklecane waited at the foot of the stairs, tapping her fingers on the brass railing with faint impatience. Fiona breathed in deeply as she walked down the old steps. She was glad that none of the other children had seen her, and she wanted to leave rather than risk meeting any of them.

A boot fell from the loose bundle and clattered down the stairs. Dame Cracklecane caught it and asked, "Well, did you get everything?" Fiona nodded, hastily tucking the boot into her cloak. "The necessary arrangements are all settled under the Law," she went on, holding the door open for Fiona. "You are now the ward of Harrow Hall. I hope you'll be happy with us, my dear."

The coach was waiting for them in the courtyard. Brown

leaves mottled with dark yellow and rust were strewn over the cobblestones like the tatters of a patchwork quilt, rustling as the two of them walked to the coach. The horses whickered restlessly, and the sun seemed to hesitate, making the world pale and thin as morning mist. Fiona blinked, and the autumn sunlight made the world real once more, leaving her to shake her head in bewilderment.

What just happened? She frowned, handing her bundle of belongings to the coachman. She stamped one foot on the worn gray cobblestones. Solid as ever...but everything looked as if it could be wiped away with a damp rag. No! The world is more real than that, isn't it?

Dame Cracklecane helped her into the light coach. "The servants will have tea and cakes for us," she said, wrinkling her nose at the smell of hot porridge in the air. "I simply don't understand how children can stand that gruel, much less thrive upon it."

"Harrow Hall?" asked the coachman, doffing his battered black cap to Dame Cracklecane. She nodded, stepping into the coach and latching the door. He gave lumps of hard honey to his two horses, briskly rubbing their manes. "We'll have you back before the noon bells."

"There's no need to hurry," said Dame Cracklecane. The coach rattled over the cobblestones. "Fiona, would you enjoy a leisurely ride through town?"

"I don't know," Fiona said, looking back at the walls of Balestone House. "I've never had one, unless you include the wagon that brought us to the workhouse."

"I shouldn't joke about such things, not so long as you dwell at Harrow Hall," said the woman. "Lethan believes that the workhouses benefit Lockhaven. He would not care to hear otherwise, my dear."

"He should work in one of them, and then he wouldn't be so sure of himself," retorted Fiona, recalling the long hours she had spent in one of the dank workhouses. "He has little notion of what it's like, working in those filthy cellars for pittance and poor health." —Her father had always said that.

"I'm quite sure it was dreadful," Dame Cracklecane said with obvious distaste. "But you needn't go back, so why does it trouble you now? You shouldn't dwell on such things, not with so much before you, my dear."

Fiona recalled that the woman had spoken of being born among the poorest folk of the country. She plainly did not want to be reminded of her origins, choosing instead the distinction of nobility conferred by the gift of The Lady. Fiona decided to say nothing more to her. The one who should be told such things was the Marl of Harrow.

The coach rattled down the slate road through the apple orchard, passing the workers at the cider press, which helped support Balestone House. Some of the workers were children, but most were penniless farmers whose lands were condemned in the plague, and who could not find work in Lockhaven. Their lives were eked out from day to day, for most of them refused to settle on the land that had been cleared at the border of the Witchwood.

What would her father be doing if he had lived? Fiona leaned back in the quiet sunlight that filled the coach. She could taste crushed apples and brine in the wind. The farm had been his life. She would not want to see him begging for work in Lockhaven. Her mother would have loathed it. Both would have been lost in the world beyond the farm.

Fiona recalled the farmhouse in autumn, with dead leaves blowing about the slate roof and green shutters. It was time to gather the alder branches and weave the Brown Man. Father would place the traditional figure in the stubbled field, and her mother would cut it into eight pieces that were scattered in the eight directions. Then there would be cider and songs around an enormous bonfire with the hired hands, watching the antlered moon rise over the hills. It was the same for every farm between the Three Towns and the Watchwall. The bonfires made the countryside blaze as if hundreds of stars had fallen in one night.

Fiona realized that the plague had only hastened the end of that rustic way of life, for in the past years most of the farms had been bought by the Gentry. The Corn Tithe had been raised after the defeat of the People of the Stallion Banner. There were few who could bear this increased burden, although some had called for the founding of a protective Grange. Her parents were among them, and much could have been achieved if it had not been for the plague, which had only served to uphold the interests of the Gentry.

Now most of the remaining farmers labored for others on the land that had belonged to them, sharecropping rather than working in the mills of Lockhaven. There was no longer talk of the Grange.

The coach bounced over loose slate. Fiona knew that it was useless to dwell upon what might have been, but she could not help herself. Her parents would hardly have approved of her living at Harrow Hall. But it was her life, and she must make her own choices now.

The slate road followed the edge of the crumbling chalk cliffs. She could hear the cries of hungry gulls, soaring in the brine and breeze. The waves below gnawed and pounded at the rocks, putting her in mind of those smugglers who chanced both wreckage and the gallows to defy the law. Some farmers had chosen that life in order to pay the Corn Tithe.

Fiona sat up and glanced out the window of the coach as they gradually approached Lockhaven. Its battered gray walls loomed over rolling meadows of sweet grass and heather. The walls and huge gates of oak and bronze were the last remnants of the fortress that slowly grew into the town of Lockhaven. Although the gates were always open now, there were cannon on the battlements that dominated both land and sea. Clouds of spray made the air glisten over the edge of the cliffs, where the Cairwell River divided the town before tumbling into the gulf below in an immense waterfall, thundering and foaming in ceaseless rage. Fiona could see the shimmering rainbow that arched over the massive walls as the coach drew closer to the town, and she glimpsed the banners of rust and cloth-of-gold that snapped from the towers crowned with bronze, glinting in the sun.

"I've never seen it like that," she murmured, gazing at the town with wide eyes, its colors clearer and brighter than any she had ever seen. She laughed with delight. "It looks like a stained glass window, but made out of jewels, with the sun blazing just behind it!"

"Lethan would be very pleased to hear that," said Dame Cracklecane. "Lockhaven is what his family made out of ruins and warring clans. They chose to settle in these lands rather than plunder them, as their folk had done for many years. He strives to uphold that heritage, although some wonder if it is still to the good of Lockhaven." She sighed. "So much is changing these days!"

Fiona nodded without hearing her, absorbed in the vision of beauty and strength that was Lockhaven. She watched as the cowherds and white cottages slipped past the coach like froth on the meadows. The rows of tall white birches that lined the slate road shone in the sun, their crowns daubed with autumn. Soldiers in green and brown could be seen upon the battlements of the town, while scarlies wheeled in the bright morning sky above them.

The clear sunlight became cool shadow as the coach rode through one of the huge gates, where farmers had raised their thatched stalls. There were fewer than in the old days, but there were still cabbages, turnips, beans and squash. Herds of pigs and goats milled about the gate, despite the

efforts of herdsmen to move them; fat geese perched on
the slate roof of an alehouse, honking at the boy who
climbed after them on an old ladder, while several men
cheered him on with frothing tankards of brown ale. A
harpist unloaded bales of hay from a wagon, earning his
daily bread beside two men in the plain harhide and shell
ornaments of distant Tuola. It had become common for
southrons to seek work in the Three Towns. Scarce har-
vests and scant tithes had ruined many of the small towns
of the southland, already bled weak by years of war.

Fiona caught her breath as a woman came walking
through the crowd, clad in riding breeches and jerkin of
doeskin, her chestnut hair plaited with gold into a ponytail.
Her mantle was the black of the cavalry, distinguished by
two slashes of cloth-of-gold lightning; buckled at her hips
were pistol and sword, each worked with onyx and red
gold, along with pouches of powder and lead shot. Her
features and bearing were both assured, with wry laughter
curling the edge of her mouth.

Fiona recognized her even as the soldiers in the throng
saluted her fist-over-heart. She was the Marl of Ciaran,
and it was her leadership that turned the tide of battle
against the People of the Stallion Banner. Morwenna
Brightflower had commanded the Host-of-War in nine
days of unending battle at the gates of Lockhaven. The
vaunted muskets and iron swords alone were not enough
without her courage and shrewd mind in the face of that
overwhelming horde out of the Plains of Har. She was
known to have slain seven chieftains in hand-to-hand battle, and although such tales often grew in the telling, in
this instance it was the truth. There were few so respected
by their foes.

A boy walked up behind her, clad in simple hunting
garb of quilted tunic and breeches, his attentive features
so like hers that he must be her son. The single difference

was the streak of bronze in his unruly chestnut hair, un-
restrained by his leather headband, which trailed several
gull feathers in the manner of the sea-tribes of Sorl.

They joined the soldiers, sharing tankards of brown ale
with them. The boy happened to glance at the coach, his
chin speckled with foam, and he smiled at Fiona. She bit
her lip in embarrassment. He looked no more than fifteen,
but in his bearing she saw an assurance that made him
older. The scars of tusk and spear showed upon his tanned
forearms. He smiled once more, and this time she smiled
back.

The coach moved on, and she settled back in her seat
as they rode out through the huge gate. The bronze domes
of the gray towers burned in the sun above them like the
lighthouse of Eádnarr. The cobblestone street led through
the center of town, crowded with shops and inns, but she
knew that most of the alleys led to the workhouses and
the rows of slate hovels in which the poor lived under the
looming walls. There were dozens of alehouses in that part
of town, bustling each night with workers who sought to
forget their long day in the gray mills, spending their wages
on ale and the gaming boards. It was an enormous pot
that was kept boiling by the frustration and anger of those
who did not share in the burgeoning wealth of the Three
Towns.

Fiona was sure that it would not be long until the pot
finally boiled over. It was true that none went hungry these
days, but the penniless wanted more than scraps. There
had already been riots started by the followers of the ubiq-
uitous King Clodde. Hangings had been of little use in
putting an end to his following, which grew after each riot.
Her father would surely have joined their ranks.

They passed the white stone walls and black shutters of
a printing shop, its black door embossed with the golden
seal of Harrow. Sheafs of broadsides and pamphlets were

set into print for the masses in such shops. The number of people who could read was growing, much to the dismay of the Gentry.

Perhaps she should learn how to read, especially if the powerful did not approve of it. She was no longer living at the orphanage, where it had been forced upon her. There was no need to spite herself now.

"You look very determined," said Dame Cracklecane. Her eyes narrowed with curiosity. "I hope that nothing troubles you, my dear."

"Nothing is wrong," answered Fiona. She heard the slow thunder of the waterfall, saw the air filled with billows of icy spray, as the coach drew near the immense bridge that arched in granite and black oak across the Cairwell River. She felt the bridge shake as its pillars were battered by the surging river, but there were strong bones of cedar and bronze within those pillars, and the huge bridge had withstood the torrent of froth and fury for centuries. There were dwellings carved into the largest pillars, their thick windows level with the foaming water, where scholars chose to work in solitude. She wondered what it was like to live over the seething cauldron of the waterfall, hearing nothing but the endless roar of the river through the walls, working upon ancient scrolls as the water rose over the windows. It was difficult to imagine how one could sleep without dread in Bridging Hall.

She could barely see the jagged firth through the spray, but she glimpsed the white sails of a whaling ship as it departed upon its voyage of three years, the warm sun spreading like oil on the waves before it. Gulls drifted in its wake, waiting for the scullery boy to dump the bucket of slops. Fiona snorted. Father always said that most people got little more than the slops, because the bucket was owned by the Gentry.

What was the alchemy that changed the dross of lives to

the purest gold? She mulled over it, watching the ship catch a northerly wind, bearing it past the guardian lighthouse of Eádnarr. Then it was bounding with strained sails across the coastal currents and into the open sea, pennants snapping in the wind. Fiona suddenly longed to be on that ship, escaping from all that had happened.

The coach left the bridge, and before them appeared the sprawling estates of the Gentry. Each was an ancient fortress of gray stone and black oak mantled with ivy, rising up from fields of heather. The boundaries were marked by low walls of fitted stones and trimmed hedgerows, and in the distance was the crumbling bulk of the Brandwall. Its ruins stretched from the chalk cliffs to the edge of the Witchwood. The remnants of towers were guarded by enormous stone lions, and the bronze shields that had blazed with warning brands still gleamed in the sun.

So this was the domain of the Gentry. It was quiet and pastoral, the clear streams dappled with brown leaves falling from the misty apple groves, with packs of lean dogs bred to arrogance lolling in the heather. There was tranquillity born of power in the air.

Harrow Hall stood proudly beneath the very eaves of the Witchwood. Its outer walls sagged under ivy and nettles; the bars of the iron gate rattled with rust. Sweetwater gleamed drowsily among tall yellow reeds, and tame swallows flickered across a field of pea grass. Scathlings camped in the shade of damp willows, roasting geese over coals, their iron swords unsheathed and close at hand.

"Here we are," Dame Cracklecane said as the coach drew up to the main house. Its slate roof was scattered with red leaves, and twining vines of gold filigree glinted from the dark green shutters. "This will be your home, my dear."

Fiona looked at the black oak doors, embossed with the golden seal of Harrow. She stepped from the coach, spitting three times through her front teeth for luck. The coachman chuckled and fetched her belongings. This was now her home. She must make the best of it.

Greylock brushed back his coarse black hair, its single lock of dull silver ignored by the morning sun. The crown of the forest loomed over him, an enormous wave of somber green spattered with russet and bronze, soughing ceaselessly in the autumn wind. He was not comforted by the sunlight, not this close to the encroaching Witchwood.

He patted the rump of his bony horse, yellow leaves blowing over his patched brown garb. "You'll wait for me, hmm?" he muttered. The horse snorted wearily. "Well, this doesn't concern you, old bag-o'-bones," he added, taking up his staff of gnarled hawthorn. "You just wait here, dreaming of fresh oats and sweet hay. I'll do what needs doing." He shook his head. "Why must this nonsense fall to me?"

He waded through drifts of leaves toward the cottage at the edge of the forest. His craggy face was troubled, for all his grumbling words. He was being drawn back into the world he had forsaken so many years ago, and bitter memories stirred in the green depths of his eyes, floating with flecks of wan gold. But he could not turn away now.

Moss stained the white stone walls of the cottage, and the chimney had been shattered by lightning one summer. Rows of beanpoles led to the oaken doors of a root cellar, their bronze hinges crusted with verdigris; ivy crept over the bark shingles of a withy shed. The stillness was gently dappled with patches of sunlight.

Greylock leaned upon his staff. The stone had been set in a bed of wild thyme. "Maeve...Awin..." He whispered the names carved into the stone along with flowering vines and leaves of willow. "I've come home...."

He listened for their voices, but the gusting of leaves was all that he heard in the wind. The morning sun shivered over the bed of wild thyme in silence, pale with autumn. He abruptly turned away and went to the withy shed.

The doors were little more than slabs of bark, sagging on hinges of tin scraps. He opened the loose doors, stepping through cobwebs and wisps of sunlight. The paint was faded and peeling from the wagon, but its legend was still plain to see in ornamental red letters: THE GREAT GREYLOCK. Puppets dangled on strings of silver, their features at once delicate and grotesque. Dust breathed dimly into the air as he took one from its peg.

"Gernie the Witchwife." He frowned, looking at the face of the ogress that time and ignorance had made of Ygerna, the last queen of Therrilyn. Children still went to bed in fear of the pallid hag who came in the night to slowly drink their blood, her white kirtle blotched black with the decay of the grave. Gwyneth had always detested this bogey, for it mocked the heritage she had found for herself.

He placed the aged puppet back upon its peg. There was no use putting off his distasteful task. He raised his staff and trudged into the Witchwood.

The earth was soft with the mold of fallen leaves that had lain untouched for countless seasons. The air was strong with it, and each deep breath fortified him like the wine he dared not drink. Beards of moss dripped from the branches of massive oaks. He clutched his staff tightly as the glinting pool came into view.

It was edged with thick ferns and yellow reeds, but the water was clear of the fallen leaves that should have covered it. A slab of gray stone lay at the middle of the pool, its weathered face carved with runes, and damp sunlight fell upon it through the mossy branches. There were mounds of cracked bones at the bottom of the pool, and the shards of old bronze weapons were scattered among them.

He thrust his staff into the still pool. "Hear me, Old One!" he called, splashing the water to froth. "I would have your rede!"

The voice that groaned from the depths of the pool was frightful with the weight of untold centuries in darkness and solitude. "I know the weaving of the spider's web, and the secrets written in the owl's wing, and the tongues uttered at the earth's roots, and the wrath of lightning's stroke." A shuddering ripple coursed through the pool, and the huge slab of gray stone shook as if something lay trapped beneath it. "What would you know, manling?"

Greylock leaned wearily upon his staff. "I would know of the blood offerings in the alder groves," he demanded. "I would know of the mills that grind men's bones into meal for the bread of Holdir. I would know of the witch's supper upon the chalk mounds." He was startled by the rustling of dead leaves in the wind. "I have seen these things, and more than these things," he said, feeling as if the long branches were about to reach down and tear at him. "What is happening, Old One?"

"I am bound in the darkness and thus have no choice but to serve you, manling." The clear waters began to cloud with blood. "The bonds are weakening, and my brethren shall soon be loosed upon this world, to serve Ygerna!" The man stepped back from the pool. "Why do you blench? The oracles of the alder twigs and bird's bones have prophesied it, and such old ways are more to be trusted than the runes of Haldir. There is nothing to be done, manling."

"I have seen enough blood spilt across this land," said Greylock. "Who would spill more? What are their names, Old One? I will have them if it means your destruction!" The bloodied water rippled with laughter, for his threat was hollow. Yet the bonds compelled an answer nonetheless, and he smiled grimly. "You will tell me, Old One."

The slab of gray stone lurched upward and then settled

back into the water. "You know them. Helskarth...
Gwyneth...Helmeric...." The voice began to dwindle into
the rippling of the pool. "You have taken my rede, and
you shall now take my curse, whether it be upon your head
or the flesh of your flesh, manling!"

Greylock shook his head with bitter amusement. "I have
cursed myself more surely than you could hope, Old One."
The autumn light carved anguish into his weathered face.
"There is nothing worse you can do to me now. You may
rot and dream of vengeance in your prison!"

He turned on his heel and stamped through the drifting
yellow leaves, until he was out of the forest. His knuckles
were white on the bole of his staff, and sweat ran down
the lines of his face. It had been too long for him. He
caught his breath. Icy knots tightened in his belly. He was
more shaken than he had expected. The branches seemed
to rub one another like satisfied fingers, and he could not
be sure if it was merely the wind.

"You waited for me, eh?" he muttered, leading his horse
to the withy shed. "Well, this may be burdensome, but no
one will take any notice of a puppeteer's wagon." He hitched
up his horse, fumbling with the buckles and straps. "I
doubt if any will remember the Great Greylock."

The dangling puppets rattled on their pegs as he drove
the wagon out of the shed. The sun was warm on his face,
and he raised one hand over his eyes, looking out upon
the rich countryside sprawling before him.

He saw meadows strewn with red mallow and linsey,
their fragrance mingling with the smoke of peat fires, and
stubbled fields marked by hayricks. There were villages of
black oak and fitted stone, built snugly in tiny dells; the
ruins of an old tower, its bronze crown encrusted with
years; the lonely cottages of drovers, their pastures of sweet
grass edged with blackthorn. Wild geese flew over the
marshes, their shadows whispering in yellow reeds. Wil-

lows sighed among the heather and headstones of the Haugh.

The country was peaceful, for the prophecies had become little more than doggerel, and there were few who believed in them. Children sang the old lines while playing games, such as Bobbing-the-Broom or Step-by-Step. Perhaps some wandering minstrel spun strands of lore into his ballads, but that was merely filigree of gold. Folk were practical, and had no use for prophecies, which were thin and feathery as the stuff of clouds.

Yet there were blood offerings in the alder groves, and the witch's supper had been eaten upon the chalk mounds. How could such foul practices go on, untroubled by the vengeance of the Mark?

Greylock slowly rubbed the bones of his neck, pondering over the familiar names dredged out of the Old One. What was he supposed to make of them?

Helskarth was said to brood in disquieting rule over the moors and maple woods of Falcondale. Gwyneth would be at her spinning wheel in the quiet village of Dyrning. Helmeric was dead, but there was his family in Lockhaven.

He could see the bronze towers of the town, glinting in the morning sun. "Let's be on our way," he frowned, snapping the knotted reins. "It may already be too late."

The wagon crackled heavily through drifts of leaves. He settled into the broken wicker seat. Rushe would never listen to him. He must speak with her sons, if she had not poisoned them with her hatred of the Mark. There was no time to search out the others. Falcondale was too distant, and he could not bear to confront Gwyneth. There was no other choice but to go to Lockhaven.

Four

"THIS IS YOUR ROOM NOW," said Dame Cracklecane, opening the massive oak door. "I've done
what could be done with it. I hope that you like it."

There were heavy drapes of green velvet drawn back
from the windows, and the morning sun blazed in warm
gold upon the floor, now covered with an enormous brown
bearskin. A sheaf of reeds hung over the bed, which was
almost lost in the soft fleecy mass of a dark green quilt.
The hems of the quilt were woven with vines and leaves
of gold, and dried herbs were sewn into its corners for
good fortune. Candles stood in lamps of antique pewter
upon the bed-table, along with a cedar box of matches.
There were four oak and brass chests of clothing below
the windows, one for each season of the year. It was a
comforting room.

The painting still hung over the warm hearth, the three
children standing knee-deep in ferns, the sun of past days
at their backs. Dame Cracklecane looked away from it.

"The servants will attend to your clothes and the linen,
of course," she went on warmly. Fiona hesitantly walked
into the room. Her room. "You'll find the washings just
down the hall. Now, if there is anything else you should
need, merely ring for the servants."

Fiona carelessly tugged at the long cord of green velvet
which had been pointed out to her, and jumped back as
the low chiming of bells came through the wall.

"I didn't mean to do that," she said, her face red with

embarrassment. She hastily released the cord. "It was just an accident."

"There's no need for apologies," said Dame Cracklecane. She shook her head as the girl fidgeted her feet. "You must grow accustomed to living in the manner of the Gentry." She smiled. "It's not so dreadful, my dear. You might enjoy it before long."

"I really don't need any servants," Fiona said, looking at the cord. She was starting to feel out of place now. "I wouldn't know what to say to them. I never liked waiting on others, so..." She shrugged her shoulders, distaste in the gesture. "I just don't need any servants."

Dame Cracklecane regarded her with an amused glance and said, "Very well." She walked to the oaken chests below the windows and placed her hand on a bundle of red velvet, woven with leaves of gold. "I saved this for you, if you wondered where it was, my dear."

She unwrapped the bundle, revealing the bronze sword of the Stallion Banner. It was speckled with dried mud, but the antlered moon carved at the base of the blade glinted in the morning sun. Fiona shivered with a disdainful chill. It was just like a thick-witted southron to invoke bad luck by using the sign of Holdir! She sighed in exasperation. Although it did look rather fearsome...

Dame Cracklecane smiled at the girl, drawing one finger along the filigree of alder leaves that was finely cut in the sword. Silver fire burned as fleetingly as sparks.

"You should learn how to wield this," she said, turning to Fiona. "Bronze in hands such as ours will prevail against iron and witchspawn." The cold ringing of her voice left no doubt that she had prevailed against both, and that blood had often stained her slim hands. "You possess the strength and the power of the Fire. You lack only the skill, and that you will learn soon enough, my dear." She gently laughed. "But not without bruises and aching bones in plenty, unless you're another Birle Keldárin! Not that she was ever one of us, of course; we are not the only ones to have carved out legends." She turned to the tall windows, staring uneasily at the edge of the Witchwood. "Legends are often misleading, as you will learn once you enter the Mark."

"There really is such a thing?" Fiona said, craning her neck to glance out the window. She stopped before she could be noticed by the brooding woman. "It's not just a legend?"

Dame Cracklecane laughed. "You still have doubts, even after feeling the touch of the Fire?" She stepped away from the windows. The sword glinted brightly on the folds of red velvet. She trailed her fingers over the hilt. "You didn't speak of this to your friends—?"

"What friends?" Fiona said sourly. "No, not a word of it." She picked at the white buttons of her kirtle, fearing that she had admitted too much already, and hastily laughed at herself. "No one would ever believe me, anyway!"

"I'm quite sure of that." Dame Cracklecane frowned, her eyes shining with bitterness and loss. "There are still some who would cart us off to the fire-pit as witchwives, even in this fine day, for most folk confuse Witcherie with the way of The Lady." She nervously tossed her head. "You should know the difference before you join the Mark. Witcherie is nothing more than whoring after power for one's own purposes, rather than wielding it for The Lady. Such foulness has no place in the Mark." Her pale brow glistened with beads of sweat, and she seemed to struggle for her words. "You must never forget this, my dear!"

She turned to the tall windows, her black hair gleaming in the sunlight. "We have labored to stamp out that foulness for many years, only to be tarred with the same brush." Her fingers tapped unevenly on the stone sill, graven with leaves of hawthorn. "Witcherie was broken, but folk still lived in fear of its leavings—dreadful, witless things! You've heard of Roke Wyndirél? He was one of us, and his greatest battle was against such witchspawn. And those who betrayed him were witching-folk."

Dame Cracklecane watched the dead leaves gusting across the heather, her troubled face reflected in the window like a ghost. "The tales speak only of his might as a warrior, and forget his fealty to The Lady," she murmured. "The good that we have done is forgotten, or it is claimed for Haldir. —But enough of this maundering! The prophecies shall be fulfilled before long...." She touched the diamond panes, closing her fingers into a bony knot. The glass rattled loudly, and then she lowered her trembling hand. "There's no going back from what's been done," she said at last. "We must look to what's before us, my dear."

She abruptly clasped the bronze sword. "This blade was forged on the Plains of Har," she said, using her fingernails to scrape off the dried mud. "It's unforgiving country, and it breeds unforgiving folk. I've seen entire villages put to the torch, and for no other reason than to slay witchwives." Her eyes were distant. "The Age of the Axe never did come to an end in that country, and it probably never will, not with those horse-tails running loose! They've little better to do than guzzle ale and lop off heads like so many gourds!" She put down the sword. "I've walked that country, my dear."

"What made you do that?" Fiona asked, biting her lip in bewilderment. There must be some canker gnawing away at Dame Cracklecane! She would have asked what it was, but instinct made her keep silent. "The Plains of Har!" she continued too loudly, and looked up at the painting over the hearth. "I'd never go there, not for all the pearls in Niane!"

Dame Cracklecane smiled wanly, but her eyes were narrow and grim. "There is a city called Pel Lendwrei," she

said as drifting clouds chilled the room. "No one has walked
in its courts since it was overwhelmed by Bain Lackwit. It
was long ago swallowed up by the Witchwood." Sunlight
poured through the windows in the wake of the clouds,
but the room was still uncomfortably cold. "I wasn't that
much older than you when we went there, following tales
of abandoned treasure, all for the sake of the Mark. There
were twenty in our company, but only four of us returned
from those ruins, each of us bearing scars in our own
fashion. We battled gaunts, and worse than gaunts. There
were horrors that still lingered from the fall of Witcherie."
She closed her eyes, clasping her pale hands at her breast.
"Oh, the arrogance of youth burned within our hearts,
stronger even than the Fire! We mocked the legends, and
in our pride thought only of power, not The Lady. And
so our companions were slaughtered like so many terrified
sheep by that lurking spawn of Witcherie. But four of us
fled with our lives, which had been spared by The Lady."

The morning bells tolled in the distance, and she opened
her eyes to the present. "I don't mean to frighten you,"
she said, smiling warmly at Fiona. "I merely want you to
realize the full meaning of your heritage, for there is much
foulness lingering in this world, and we must always protect
unknowing folk from it." She could not hold back the
bitterness in her voice. "We do this, although most folk
would either scorn us or condemn us. But they are too
learned to believe in us, or it! Folk must believe what they
will, and there's nothing to be done about it. I simply hope
that you won't be frightened off, my dear."

Fiona looked at the bronze blade, glinting on the folds
of velvet. Dame Cracklecane truly expected her to wield
that against witchspawn. Yet she was not frightened, for
she had difficulty in imagining it. The orphanage had
taught her not to believe in legends.

Well, if the orphanage was against it, then she was for

it! And she was quite familiar with scorn. Perhaps that was the canker gnawing away at Dame Cracklecane. Scorn could be more terrible than festering wounds. But none of that really mattered to her now. She had been offered the chance to put those days in the orphanage behind her, and she would not let that chance slip through her hands. It was only sensible to join the Mark.

"I won't be frightened off," she said, clasping the goad in her pocket. What else could she really do? "It's what my family would have wanted, isn't it?"

Dame Cracklecane paled, but she did not hesitate to nod her head. "Yes, of course," she said firmly, stirring up the ashes in the hearth. "I know that your mother was certainly devoted to The Lady." The iron poker clattered loudly as she dropped it into the rack. "But you mustn't make this choice for your family. It must be for yourself, my dear."

"I'm sure that it's the best thing," Fiona replied, her fingers tightening on the goad. She could taste wild rose in the air, and something tingled at the nape of her neck. "It was good of you to tell me about the Mark. I'm quite sure of my choice now."

"Very good." Dame Cracklecane wrapped the bronze blade up in the swatch of velvet. "Bring this with you," she said, handing the bundle to Fiona. "It's time you started on your lessons."

"I'm ready for them," Fiona said, smiling as she tucked the sword into the crook of her arm. Dame Cracklecane smiled back, her eyes filled with wry amusement. There was no need to say anything. But this silence was much too uncomfortable for Fiona. "I wasn't very good at my lessons before—I mean in the orphanage—" She bit her lip. "I'll try to do better with these, though!"

Dame Cracklecane led her down the halls, stopping before an oak door bound in tarnished silver, its cracks bearded with moss. There was only one tall window in the passage, clouded with years of dust. Yet the air seemed to breathe with silver wherever one looked, and the runes carved upon the door shone dimly as stars. Fiona rubbed the nape of her neck, which felt like an icy lump. It grew almost painful as she walked up to the waiting door, but she did not want to seem frightened, and so she said nothing to Dame Cracklecane.

"Well, here we are," the woman said, taking a silver key from her pocket. "I first unlocked this door more than twenty years ago, when most of this passage was still overgrown with the Witchwood. Lethan's father cleared it all out, every leaf and twig." She smiled to herself, turning the key in the old lock. "Helmeric was always very thorough, no matter how small the task. —Ah, that's got it! Come inside, my dear."

The chamber had been hewn from obsidian, and the massive arches that supported the dome of the ceiling glinted with red veins of gold. Hinged panels of oiled hardwood concealed the many alcoves, after the fashion of the Scathe. The windows were simply panes of pebbled amber, held together with bronze filigree and mounted on frames of black oak. The sun spreading over the slate floor was like the palest of honey. It touched all but the antiquated loom by the far wall, cobwebbed with an unfinished tapestry.

Dame Cracklecane placed an old-fashioned cobbler's bench beside the floor hearth. "Please sit down," she said, folding a heavy fleece over the bench. "It's fitting that you should study in here, for these very walls were carved in the days of Therrilyn." She opened one of the windows, and the fragrance of mown heather filled the room. "Oh, it's lovely outside! I hope you don't mind staying in, my dear."

"I should be starting my lessons." Fiona smiled, looking over the fleece for nits before sitting down. She knocked her knees together, holding the bundled sword in her lap. "Well! I'll certainly do my best!" Dame Cracklecane gave her another amused smile, and Fiona feared that she sounded like some goosy little girl. She decided to say nothing more, and fidgeted on the bench.

"I'm sure that all of this is unsettling, and just a bit silly in the morning sun," Dame Cracklecane said, lingering at the open window. "That's how it seemed to me, sitting at the feet of my teacher, and my head stuffed with all the wisdom of thirteen years! I don't expect you to believe everything all at once, so you needn't worry about that; simply do your best, and you'll do just fine, my dear. Please get it through your head that this isn't the orphanage! I would like us to be friends. Do give me that chance, Fiona."

The wind stirred her finely braided hair, sweeping up the raven's wing like a banner in the sun. Fiona suddenly felt an ache tightening in her throat. But there was nothing that she could say to Dame Cracklecane.

The woman gave an exasperated sigh as she sorted through the alcoves, her sleeves rolled up to her elbows. "We'll need some fennel wine," she said, turning to Fiona. "I'll have to fetch a bottle from the cellar. This won't take very long, so wait for me, hmm?"

Fiona listened to her brisk footsteps dwindling down the hall. She looked about the room, wondering if the fennel wine was merely an excuse to leave her alone with her doubts. Not that there was any reason for it. She should be enjoying what she had gained through luck or The Lady. Yet it was not that simple, for she did not feel comfortable with the fine life of the Gentry.

The bronze sword glinted on the fleece, and she brushed the folds of red velvet. The rich cloth was ruined by mud and moss. She shook her head in disgust. Her family could never have afforded such cloth, and here it was carelessly used like an old rag. How could she enjoy this arrogance? Her father would have walked scornfully away from it!

But her father was dead, and there was no use struggling to do what he would have wanted—or what her mother would have wanted, for that matter. Dame Cracklecane was right. It had to be her own choice. Yet she still felt guilty, and that was enough to fill her with doubts.

She wrapped the fleece about her shoulders like a cloak and walked to the open window. Sunlight fell on her freckled face. She could see the crown of the forest, its dark green leaves edged with bronze and rust. The breeze tasted of damp pine needles and woodwash. Squirrels were gathering nuts in the fallen leaves, and wild geese were already winging toward the southland.

Fiona looked down at the squared field of pea grass just below the window, where servants were busy raking up mounds of leaves, their faces brown as dried bark. One had stopped for a long drink of cider, splashing his ragged tunic as he hefted the jug. He saw her and grinned, even as more leaves rustled by him in a gust of wind. He brandished his wide rake with an exaggerated bellow of dismay. It was not so terrible to work at Harrow Hall.

Scathlings camped in the grove of willows beyond the pea grass, setting themselves apart from the servants. There were children climbing in the branches of a huge willow, but their mothers did not seem concerned, for they were engrossed in the sewing of a patchwork quilt. The men tended to their horses, their swords, and the family wagons. Scathlings had their own notions of propriety, and it was unusual for such narrow folk to serve one of the Gentry. Fiona could not make any sense of it. Well, how much sense could one get out of southrons? It probably had something to do with Lethan.

Fiona leaned upon the ledge with her elbows, cupping

her chin in her hands. What would it be like, wandering the length of the land? Those southrons might eventually journey as far as Nethernesse. Folk were said to live by hunting and trapping in that frozen country, especially prizing the white pelts of snow-apes—who were said to walk the icebound crags with knives of flint, taking the scalps of all who were unlucky enough to cross their path. But such tales were probably so much nonsense, since all northrons learned to lie before they could walk. Fiona had never met one, but she had heard all the tales about them.

She turned away from the window, rubbing her fingers on the pebbled amber panes until they tingled, her gaze wandering idly about the chamber walls. Her reflection looked back at her from the polished obsidian. She barely recognized herself in the fine clothes of the Gentry. The warm tingling in her fingers seemed to spread through her body, and she swirled her kirtle with embarrassed delight. But she felt too plain and skinny to go on pretending, as she considered it. Let another girl play the numbwit!

She began to poke about in the alcoves, folding back the hinged panels like a thief. There was nothing much of interest in the first few, but she was stopped short by the remains of a tapestry. It was hanging upon a wooden frame, as if someone wished to repair it.

She could discern the brooding face of a young man, his black hair tousled with a single lock of bronze, and a sprig of hawthorn over one ear. The berries had been rendered red as blood. The rest had been ruined by a slashing knife, but she could see that the eyes were green, swimming with flecks of gold. The Mark! But something else nagged at her, as if she had seen the face before, or one very like it.

She heard loud footsteps ringing down the hall, and she hastily replaced the hinged panel, leaving the alcove just as she had found it. Then she sat down, her fingers clasped in her lap.

"Well, that didn't take so long," Dame Cracklecane said as she opened the door, a dusty bottle of fennel wine in her hand. "Now, let's get started on your lessons."

Lethan stood before the iron gates, the bars twining with ivy, and looked up at the humble gray walls of the Abbey of Haldir. The wind gusted through his thin cloak and raised the yellow leaves about his ankles, but he took little notice of it. His pale eyes were set upon one barred window. The gray clouds hissed across the sun. He winced at the scraping of rime against the sky.

"Ye'll be going in, aye?" Egil muttered, pulling his red cloak over his burly shoulders. He set one scarred hand upon the hilt of his iron sword, glancing uneasily at the walls of the abbey. Someone was moaning in the distance. Or was that merely the wind? "I'd not choose it, Lord Harrow."

Lethan did not heed him. "She sits in that barren room each day," he said, brushing the stray leaves from his russet coat. "I've done nothing to help her, save to make her life less unpleasant." He frowned, rubbing his hands together for warmth. "I must do something, Egil."

"Ye've done a goodly lot—"

Lethan shook his head. "It's not enough," he said. The wind snapped up his words like a hungry dog. "I persist in hoping, even if there seems to be no hope. —And where's that gatekeeper?"

He angrily rang the iron bell bolted upon the gate, and the yellow leaves flinched as it tolled out rust. A flock of scarlies settled on the slate roof of the abbey. He watched them squabbling as he waited in the pale sunlight. The bones of his face seemed worn as driftwood. He rang the bell once more. Gulls drifted over the edge of the cliffs, their cries lingering in a sky wrung of color like a washrag.

A girl finally appeared from behind the gatehouse, clad in the gray kirtle of a novice, with a pair of pruning shears in one hand. Her brown hair was pulled back in a disheveled bun, and her eager face was smudged with dirt. A hornbook of simple prayers was tucked into her pocket, which was missing one of its plain buttons.

"Lord Harrow." She smiled, reaching into the gatehouse for a clattering ring of keys. "I did hear the bell, so you needn't have gone on clanging it. I was quite busy with the hedges, although mere trimming is useless. They ought to be torn up by the roots!"

She clasped the pruning shears under one arm and sorted through the keys. "I'll put the kettle on for tea if you'd care for a mug. It's plain butternut, but there's plenty of honey, and it'll warm you up." She glanced fondly at the young Marl. "It's good to see you again, my lord."

"I really haven't the time for tea just now. It's good of you to ask, though," he added gently. "I'd like to speak with my mother, Cait."

"Come in, then," she said, her restrained voice that of the gabled sugaring villages in Nethernesse. "Do you want me to fetch the Abbess? Not that she comes running at my every beck and call!" Her hazel eyes shone with wry amusement. "I must learn to guard my tongue, it seems." She turned up her nose at Egil. "And what are you grinning at, you over-stuffed bumpkin?"

Lethan chuckled with the southron. "I'll just find her myself," he said, stepping back as she unlocked the gates for him. He handed over his pistol, which she placed inside the gatehouse, according to the Law. "I don't believe that she's started her rounds quite yet."

"I don't think so," she said, holding the gates open for him. "I'll still be here when you leave. If you'd like that mug of tea then, my lord?" She bowed her head. "I'll always be here, Lord Harrow."

She locked the gates, and the two men followed the slate path that led between bristly hedges of hawthorn. Lethan was already lost in thought, ignoring the leaves that blew wildly in his face, like so many lies flung back at him. But he was done with lying, if he could only persuade his mother to give up her justified hatred of the Mark. "If only..." How easy that sounded! Much easier than actually facing his mother in the next few moments.

The gray walls of the abbey loomed above the end of the path, rooted in the boulders and fields of beans that covered the ancient grounds. Rows of willows muted the biting winds from the edge of the cliffs, but the air tasted of brine with every breath. The ruins of a stone fence sheltered beehives now, and beyond it were planked steps that led to the fishery below the cliffs. The abbey provided for its own, according to the Law.

The common school and the hospice stood on either side of the abbey, their walls newly faced with brown brick. Long stone benches were shaded by wooden awnings that rattled in the wind. The courtyards were heaped with yellow leaves, and withered reeds floated in a mossy pool with the sun.

Lethan walked up to the hospice, his fingers tightening into bony fists at the moaning from the barred windows. Egil clasped his shoulder, and he smiled wanly before knocking on the maple door. The grief in his eyes had petrified over the years, and he sometimes wondered if he simply felt it out of habit.

A slot opened in the middle of the door, and two bleary eyes looked out at Lethan. "Well, what do you want?" snapped the doorkeeper, his voice slurred with broken sleep. "Speak up, numbwit!"

"Dog, 'tis th' Marl of Harrow! Ye'll not be yapping at

him!" Egil roared furiously, pounding upon the door with his meaty fist. "Now, open th' door! Or ye'll be spitting your blood up on my sword!"

The door opened, and the doorkeeper hobbled to one side on a crutch, for he was missing his right leg. The stump was swaddled in a leather sack, and his patched garb was that of a soldier, even to the gold lion pinned on his tunic. He was one of the few to have earned that honor, minted by order of the Marl of Ciaran.

He angrily slapped his stump. "I lost this fighting the People of the Stallion Banner," he muttered, his breath reeking from ale. "Begging for drudge's work is bad enough without having to bow and scrape for some filthy southron! Go on, be about your business!"

Egil reached for his sword, meaning to gut the fool and leave his carcass for the crows. He had endured enough of the gibes and open hatred of these folk. Yet he stopped and let the iron blade slip back into its sheath—for he was not about to hang for the likes of this lumpkin! The magistrates were often too eager to uphold the Law. And they would probably be most diligent in the case of a southron.

"I'll let this go, since my mother plainly hired you out of little more than pity." Lethan frowned, shaking his head in dismay. "You might do better for yourself in a workhouse, my fellow."

"Heban's my name, if that's any of your concern. And as for your stinking workhouses—!" He spat on the floor. "I'd just as soon take a beggar's bench in town. I've lost one of my legs, but at least it was by a sword, and not one of those grinding wheelworks!" His vehemence sputtered out like a wet match. "But you lot don't care a fig, so it's no use talking about it. I lost my leg to the horse-tails. I wouldn't sell this medal to get it back, either...."

Lethan hurried down the hall, feeling ashamed of himself for no discernible reason. He was surely not responsible for every cripple and drunkard! Nor was his mother, although she tried to be—but then, she was the Abbess. And she felt only hatred for the Mark. He angrily jabbed stiff fingers through his hair, his thoughts scattering like fleas.

Egil followed after him. The drab walls were broken by windows of isinglass, and dim sunlight covered the floor like yellow dust. The air seemed cramped, muffling the echoes of their steps. Egil longed to stuff up his ears at the moaning that seeped like oily smoke through the walls. There was no hope of ignoring those witless voices. He clenched his teeth and tried to endure them.

Lethan stopped at the foot of an oaken staircase, which rose above a lattice door of glass and maple wood. The door seemed out of place, its diamond panes glowing with the softness of many candles, but the gloominess of the hall made coming here most pleasant.

He opened the door, breathing in the fragrance of mint and bayberry candles. The framed bed and plain washing table were those of any novice. The floor was dark slate, and on an iron stand was a copy of the Halter. The two windows were smudges of sunlight, their shutters folded back. The quiet glow of the candles burnished the simplicity of the room with an eloquence beyond words.

His mother sat by the window, poring over the accounts of the abbey with inky fingers. Her ornate bun of black hair was charged with silver, but her features still had the fine clarity of youth. The wisps of hair on the white nape of her neck seemed to burn in their blackness, as did the tiny mole on her curving cheek.

She looked up from the scroll in her lap. The calmness of her face accentuated her stormy blue eyes, so dark as to be almost black. "What brings you here?" She smiled, her white kirtle rustling softly as she rose to her feet. The wealstone gleaming upon her red mantle was of antique gold. "But it's good just to see you no matter what the reason," she added as she kissed his cheek. "And you also, Egil."

"Dame Merúshe." He nodded, flustered as he always was in her presence. He longed to see her unpegged hair tumble down about her shoulders in a foamy black torrent. But he knew his place in this country, which constantly reminded him that he was an unlettered Scathling.

"It will do to simply call me Rushe," she said, rolling up the scroll in her hand. "I've been called that ever since my days as a fishergirl on Sorl. It's difficult to believe that thirty years have gone by—especially with such dreadful haste!" She stopped, frowning at Lethan. "What's that ugly gilding in your hair?"

He touched his fashionable silver lock. "It's merely a bit of frippery," he said with embarrassment. "It's supposed to bring good luck."

"I'm glad your father isn't here to see you dabbling in such nonsense," she snapped, washing her inkstained fingers in a pewter basin. "You should know better, Lethan. It may be harmless in itself, but—"

"'—But it merely encourages superstition.'" He folded his arms. "I've heard all of this before, Mother. Let's not thrash it out again." It was galling to be treated like the little boy who had once clung to her strong hand. He was the Marl of Harrow!

Rushe dried her fingers with the coarse toweling of the town mills. "I don't wish to quarrel," she said, recognizing the determined thrust of his jaw. "I suppose you've come to see Elsie?"

"Yes, if that won't be too disturbing for her," he said quietly, deciding that this might be for the best. He simply hoped that his mother would listen to him. "I don't imagine that she's any better?"

Rushe shook her head. "I've begun to fear that there's

just no helping her," she said, and clasped the wealstone at her breast. "However, we mustn't give in to despair, not if we have faith in Haldir. I won't let her go, not as so many others have gone before her—" The sun trembled on her face with chilly indifference, and she abruptly shuttered the two windows. "We'll go and see your sister now."

Egil waited beneath the staircase as they walked up the worn steps. The bells of the abbey tolled out the hour, but could not drown the moaning voices from above that seemed to pick at their skin. Lethan gripped the brass railing as his mother unlocked the first door at the top of the stairs.

Elspeth sat by the barred window, her hands swaddled in quilted mittens, her unwashed hair a thicket that spilled down to the small of her back. She gazed through the bars of the window, her empty green eyes flecked with gold. The innocence that lingered in her face was like spoiled milk. It was too childish for her body, which had been clumsily arranged in the chair and then restrained with straps.

"I see that she's been painting again," Lethan murmured as he saw a canvas on the slate floor, splotched in the pale sunlight. "Do you believe it does her any good?"

"It seems to calm her after an attack," Rushe said, her voice turning flat. "Whether it does her any good is another matter. I don't always like what she chooses to paint. You may see for yourself."

He looked down at the painting on the floor. It was no more than the suggestion of an agonized face wreathed in dark flames, but its urgency frightened him. He turned away when the face began to seem familiar, stepping carefully among the jars of pigments. The cries of gulls beat mockingly against the window.

"Elsie?" he said, gently touching her cheek. The smell of her hair was thick and pungent. "Elsie, do you hear me at all?" He had been coming here for years, and she was always the same when he left. "I simply don't know how you can find the strength to see her like this every day, Mother."

"It's not always that simple, although the mere passage of time makes one stronger," Rushe said, baring the hollow of her throat as she raised her head. "Sorrow is the beginning of strength, if we will only endure it." The words were from the pages of the Halter. "This family has endured enough to temper us like forged iron."

Lethan adjusted his spectacles. "It's only sensible to endure what can't be helped," he said, confronting his mother across the room. "But there's little sense in ignoring help when it's within the reach of your hand."

"You needn't go on," Rushe said coldly, almost spitting the words at him. "You would have me go sniveling for mercy from the Mark."

"We should do whatever can be done to help Elspeth!" he retorted. "Mother, what else is left? There may be no other way to help her. Isn't that what truly matters? I can't go on seeing her like this for another ten years!" He bowed his head. "Father wouldn't have allowed her to languish for ten years without doing *something*—!"

"I should have destroyed all of his papers, rather than allowing you to delve into them," Rushe murmured, closing her eyes in resignation. "Lethan, can't you get it through your head that he died because of his meddling with the Mark? You mustn't follow his example, no matter how great your longing to help Elspeth. I love you dearly for that! You've been so good to your sister—" Her throat grew taut. "You know the anguish they've inflicted upon this family, and you can still consider asking for their help? It isn't enough that one of them butchered my sister Maeve? Nor that their tainted blood has poisoned Elspeth? Nor that his fascination with them lured your father to his destruction?" She lowered her voice, which had grown shrill. "I've lost so much, Lethan. I could not bear to lose you as well. Please, will you give me your word that you'll have nothing to do with the Mark?"

"I was only suggesting that we seek to understand these things," he replied, uselessly clenching his fists. "I won't trouble you with any of this again, Mother. You've had more than enough time to consider your decision, and no difficulty at all in living with it." He swallowed his bitterness with effort. "Please do the little you can for Elsie."

Balestone House loomed against the pale yellow smear of twilight that lingered at the edge of oncoming night. Candles shone silently through the diamond panes of the windows, and the evening bells tolled from the Three Towns. Leaves blew in the damp wind.

Greylock brought the wagon to a rattling halt. He felt the autumn chill in his bones, and each breath was a plume of frost. The scarlies huddling together along the roof of the orphanage looked like shabby old men in threadbare mantles to him. He chuckled sadly, for his own mantle had been patched until little remained of the worn homespun. He had grown too accustomed to the warmth of the Scathe. Yet he drank in the fragrance of broom pine and heather like a thirsty man. This country would always be his home, despite the suffering that haunted him.

He rubbed the nape of his neck. The bones felt brittle to his knobby fingers, and he longed for a skin of wine. The longing stirred in his belly like a worm. He shuddered, and his face grew clammy with sweat. There was still time enough to turn back. But that witless notion had been nagging like an itch ever since he passed the Watchwall.

"Enough!" he snorted, mulling over the names uttered by the Old One. "I'll do what needs doing, and be done with the lot of them!"

Lockhaven waited in the distance, more imposing than he remembered it. The stillness of evening had settled upon the towers, their bronze domes shimmering with the faintest glow of twilight. The shields of slain warriors did not hang upon the walls, as he had heard, but there was an arrogance loose in this country that would have encouraged it. Folk believed that the reins of power had been firmly grasped by the Three Towns.

This might be so, and not merely because of the defeat of the People of the Stallion Banner. It was as if lightning had blasted a rotting tree, and green saplings had sprung up from the shattered trunk. The smallest villages seemed to be building their own mills and common schools. There were not many who still followed the old ways, which had become little more than the stuff of scorn. Folk lived by knowledge these days, and they were all too proud of it.

Greylock smiled grimly, for such people would scoff at his tale of blood offerings and the witch's supper. And what if the prophecies were to be fulfilled now? Scoffing would not save these knowledgeable folk!

"What's gone wrong?" he muttered, once more rubbing the nape of his neck. "Witcherie spreading like rot, the old ways tossed out like a bucket of slops, and no sign of the Mark!" He shook his head. "Someone's gone and mucked it up! They'd better be prepared for bloodshed, for it'll be coming if the prophecies *are* fulfilled now! We'll be living in another Age of the Axe!"

The wind grew colder with the cries of stray gulls. He stiffened as their cries were suddenly pierced by a terrified scream. Leaves gusted and rasped in the twilight. And then nothing, as if a knife had silenced the scream. Dusk spilled over the cliffs like ink.

Greylock hastily lit a battered tin lantern and stepped down from the wagon. Scarlies were strewn across the evening like castoff rags, shrieking with glee. He stumbled through the heather to the edge of the cliffs, his lank hair whipping from his brow, and grimaced at the stitch in his ribs. The air was soggy with brine as he slowly caught his breath. He felt too old for this sort of thing.

The lantern sputtered, but he saw the marks of slipping feet in the wet earth. There was little else to be seen from the cliffs. The sea crashed over the rocks, shaking clods of earth and chalk into the darkness, and the wind came sweeping down like an enormous broom.

It was quite easy to guess what must have happened, but guesses were not enough for him. The gulls had fled, leaving their cries to linger in the wind. He could still hear that terrified scream. Apprehension bristled down his back. This was surely no mere accident!

He was startled as light blazed across the darkness of the waves, and then he recalled tales of the great lighthouse on Eádnarr. Cannons boomed three times as the beam scythed across the firth. He shivered, waiting for it to reach as far as the cliffs.

Greylock saw a shapeless form wedged between the broken rocks, dressed in the folded red mantle and white kirtle of a goodwife. The blotch of its face stared up at him until the waves covered it. He turned away from the blackening depths, following the path that led to Balestone House.

Five

FIONA STROLLED IN THE PEA GRASS, wearing the green and silver cloak given to her by Dame Cracklecane. She combed out her braids with languid fingers. The morning sun was light as flour. The wind was tinged with frost as it rustled in the eaves of the Witchwood.

"Heh, good morn!" called a burly Scathling. He smiled from the grove of willows, and she smiled back as she saw the glint of gold from his white teeth. He waved, returning to his work, mending a patched leather ball for the children who clustered about him in anticipation. All wore loose tunics of brown homespun and rabbit pelts.

One could grow quite fond of this new life. She chewed on a damp leaf of mint, crusted with mock honey. It was very pleasant to have no chores waiting for her, and better still to sleep late, and have eggs instead of porridge when she did get up, and top that with mounds of buttered toast smothered with strawberry jam, and then loll back in bed! For all this and much more she could thank the gift of The Lady.

Fiona sighed. Now that she knew of this gift, what was she supposed to do with it? For that matter, what was she to do with herself, even without her gift? She had been raised to make something more of her life than lazy hours, no matter how pleasant, yet she was doing nothing more than living the rich and untroubled life of the Gentry. She could never have justified any of this to her father! And she was not sure if she would have tried, for she was still filled with doubts.

She watched the children chasing each other through the leaves and shade of the willows, kicking the patched leather ball toward an oaken bucket, and she suddenly longed to join in their game of Hunt-the-Hare.

No, she decided. She was growing too old for that sort of thing. What games were played among the Gentry? She sank her hands into the deep pockets of her cloak. They probably were too complicated for her to learn. Well, she didn't care about any games! It was no game to belong to the Mark. She turned wistfully away from the noisy children.

This must be how it feels to grow up. She did not know if she cared for it, although there was certainly nothing she could do to stop it. Father had told her to enjoy childhood before it slipped away through her fingers, like the withered chaff of the harvest.

She hesitantly touched the pale embroidery of vines and leaves that glistened on her kirtle, frowning as she imagined her father's disdain. He had gone into crushing debt rather than sell his land to the Gentry. She could not help feeling ashamed of herself, although there was really no good reason for it. Things were different now.

"Fiona?"

She turned, looking down the worn cobblestone path that led to the iron gates. Deirdre waved to her in gusts of brown and honey leaves. Fiona smiled in surprise and hurried down the path, her cloak billowing about her shoulders.

"Deirdre?" She caught her breath, reaching through the rusted bars and ivy to clasp hands with the older girl. "What are you doing here?"

"You asked me to come and visit," Deirdre said, swaying nervously on tiptoes. "This isn't too soon, is it? You only moved here yesterday, but we have so much to talk about!"

The wind snarled her unbound hair and gathered up heaps

of yellow leaves at her feet. "Do you know what happened last night?" she whispered, her eyes shining with embarrassed fascination. "Goody Gulde fell from the cliffs, and some traveler found her body on the rocks below, but none of us got to see it because the waves carried it off—!" The eagerness of her voice was tinged with disappointment. "I was fetching tea for everyone last night, and no one had any notion of what she was doing on the cliffs. You should have heard them, talking of smugglers or spies or even sweethearts!" Deirdre giggled. "How could anyone want to be her sweetheart?"

Fiona bit her lip. "Goody Gulde is dead?" she murmured at last, shaking her head in disbelief. "Well, it's all that she deserved! I don't know how many times she birched me to the bone—!" Fiona looked down at her feet. "I shouldn't be so satisfied, but I can't help it," she said. "I prayed for her to die every night! I loathed her so much—! But that's heartless, isn't it?"

"No, of course it isn't," Deirdre said firmly. "We all felt the same about her, and it's not as if *we* pushed her over the cliffs." She tossed her loose hair across her shoulders and forced an uncomfortable laugh. "Let's not talk about that now," she decided. "Let's go walking, and we can talk about something more pleasant."

"What, then?"

"Oh, anything!"

Fiona unlatched the gates and tugged them open enough to squeeze through, her thin braids catching in the ivy. The raw wind stung her cheeks red as the rust that gnawed at the iron bars. Deirdre brushed the leaves from her braids for her, and she smiled with gratitude. The rusted gates creaked on their hinges, startling both of them.

They followed the low wall of fitted stones and hedges that led to the main road, looking for wizened apples in the leaves of untended groves. Scarlies blew across the

autumn sky like black rags. There was brine and mint in
the air as they cut across a field of heather, pursuing the
shadows of scudding clouds. They crossed a wide stream,
taking careful steps over mossy stones and a thick branch.
Deirdre almost slipped in her clumsy wooden shoes, and
she flailed her arms until she caught her balance. The
morning sun glistened on her teeth as she laughed, jump-
ing into the tall yellow reeds on the other side of the stream.
She settled back upon her elbows and kicked off her shoes
in lazy satisfaction. Fiona sat down beside her, arms folded
around her knees, watching gulls soar in the wind.

"This is nice," Fiona sighed, her braids dangling in the
reeds as she leaned her head back. "I wish that we could
stay like this and never grow up." She closed her eyes. "I
don't want to grow up. And yet I don't want to be treated
like a little girl." She let herself fall back into the dry reeds.
"Did you ever want different things like that, knowing that
you couldn't have both?"

"I want lots of things that can never be mine," Deirdre
replied, watching the clouds blaze from within as they
gusted across the sun. "I don't want to stop growing up,
not if it means living in *my* childhood." She rolled on her
stomach and looked at Fiona. "What were your days like
before Balestone House?"

"Oh, I used to hunt geese with my father's musket, and
sleep in an apple tree to watch the stars falling like candles
each summer, and tramp through the marsh to catch frogs,
and go skating on the pond each winter." She chewed on
a dry reed of cracklecane. "Father carved the skates from
seasoned oak and hammered the blades out of tin scraps.
He was always good with his hands. The neighbors brought
their tinkering trade to him and paid with kegs of cider
or even a day's work in our fields. He marked his work
with an odd rune like two forked twigs, and you'll find it
on every farm that lies north of the Watchwall." She

frowned. "Well, at least on the farms that weren't put to
the torch and then plowed with salt, if any are left." She
clutched the dull cattle goad in her pocket. "I don't like to
dwell on those last days."

"What of your mother?"

"It was after the defeat of the People of the Stallion
Banner," she recalled. "Father was still in the marshes with
the foot soldiers, striking at their grain encampments, and
we were alone in the farmhouse. The southrons had ignored us in their march upon Lockhaven. Now their ranks
were broken and they were falling back, hoping to reach
the gaps they had opened in the Watchwall. There were
stragglers roaming in the fields and hills, stealing geese,
sleeping in haystacks. You recall it, don't you?"

Deirdre nodded her head.

"I was in bed, and my mother was putting up preserves,"
continued Fiona. "The dogs started barking. Mother put
away her basket of strawberries and got the musket. I could
hear drunken men shouting through the shutters, coming
from behind the pigsty. Mother told me to stay in bed
while she went to the side door. She unlatched the trader's
window, raised the musket, and told whoever was there to
leave. The next thing that happened was that she shot one
of them dead. 'Now, will the rest of you louts take your
hands off those pigs and be on your way?' she shouted.
'I'll gladly shoot the lot of you if you don't!' She was re-
loading the musket, of course, and when one of them ran
at the door with his war-axe, she merely shook her head
and shot him dead as well. I could hear them swearing,
probably to stir up their courage, but none of them was
any match for my mother!"

"What finally happened?"

"They left their slain fellows in the yard and galloped
into the night," laughed Fiona. "Mother waited until she
was sure they were gone, and then went back to making

strawberry jam." She sat up and hugged her knees. "I always liked that part the best."

Deirdre bowed her head. "Your family must have been so wonderful," she murmured, her voice envious and wistful. "It was different in my home, if you could even call it that. I was a reminder to my mother that she had ruined her life, and she blamed me for that, and never let me hear the end of it. My stepfather loathed me outright, and it was all he could do to find one kind word for my mother. She only married him when it was quite plain that no one else would, for what man cared to claim another's ill-born daughter? You should have heard him brag of his goodness and sacrifice in taking me under his roof, when all he wanted was someone to help my mother clean and cook and fetch for him, which is what we did all day. He only married her for that, because he was always out whoring and drinking with his fellows. She never bothered to wait up for him. She was seldom lonely, considering the hired hands that came around to the side door. I used to stay in my room and dream of going away to school in Kelgardh."

"How awful!"

"He used to beat me for speaking of my dreams," Deirdre went on, savoring the horrified looks given her by Fiona. "I was struggling over a hornbook one day, hoping to learn some of my letters, and he grabbed it from my hands. 'Well, think you're better than me, do you?' he bellowed. 'I'll give you a lesson that you won't forget, missy!' He couldn't read his own name, and he hated anyone who knew their letters. So he took a willow switch to me until a passing soldier pounded on the door. He had heard my screaming, but my stepfather told him that he was slaughtering a sow." She spat into the clear stream. "Mother just stood there and let him do it, because she blamed me for having had to settle for him rather than an heir to the Gentry."

Fiona squirmed uncomfortably in the reeds.

"She never told me who my father was, and it's possible that she didn't know herself," frowned Deirdre, wrinkling her nose. "I've some notion of who he was, although that really doesn't matter now, since he died years ago." She tossed her head and laughed coldly. "He wouldn't have recognized me as his daughter if he had lived, so it's just as well that he is dead, isn't it?"

"I—I suppose—"

"There's no supposing about it!" Deirdre snapped as she abruptly got to her feet. "I didn't ask to be born, certainly not into my family! I wasn't blessed as you were! It isn't fair—!"

Fiona looked up at her from the reeds. "Well, it's not my fault!" she said firmly. "I'm sorry that your life hasn't been good, but you can't blame it on my life! What does one have to do with the other? I never asked to be orphaned, but it's no use blaming those who weren't responsible for my loss, don't you see?" She stood up beside the older girl. "I want us to be friends, Deirdre."

"You do?"

"Yes, very much."

Deirdre lowered her eyes. "I really didn't mean all of those things, at least not about you," she murmured, brushing the leaves from her kirtle. "I've just never had the chance to talk, not like this, and everything comes out wrong." She shook out her hair, winnowing it through her spread fingers. "No one ever wanted to listen to me before, and it's all been boiling inside of me like poison, always honeyed over with a mooncalf's smile." She stamped upon the reeds. "I'm sick to death of smiling! It's just so humiliating! And you've got to, since these are supposed to be the happiest years of your life! I absolutely loathe that! We aren't supposed to feel anything but wide-eyed innocence as we gambol in the clover—like so many sheep! It's dis-

gusting! Why must we be denied our feelings? We're just
pretty little dolls to *them!*"

Fiona clapped her hands in embarrassment. "You'd have
started an uprising if you spoke like that in the orphanage!" She laughed loudly. "We could have marched the
warders off to the gallows, and then reigned over Balestone
House!"

Deirdre smiled hesitantly. "I couldn't have borne any
cloying words of comfort just now," she said softly, jabbing
her hands into the pockets of her threadbare cloak. "Let's
go on walking."

She hastily picked up her shoes, and they followed the
stream through fields of heather rolling in from the edge
of the chalk cliffs in long, sighing swells. The wind rustled
brown and bitter orange leaves before them. Scarlies mottled the glassy sky, which was smeared with clouds like
clots of frozen milk, their bellies tinged pale yellow.

The stream ran among tall reeds and ferns, sweeping
the dead leaves of willows to the sea. Hidden in the sagging
willow branches was a shabby wagon, its gaudy colors faded
and splashed with mud. Puppets dangled from their strings
like a brace of pheasant, and the large shutters had been
unfolded to reveal a painted landscape of misty green hills
and farms, with pale clouds that resembled faces above
them.

"Well, look at that!" said Deirdre. "This is the wagon
that brought us the sad news of poor Goody Gulde!" She
looked about in anticipation. "Now, where is the driver?
He could tell us everything that happened!"

Fiona looked at the puppets, pausing uneasily over that
of a goodwife. Perhaps it was merely her imagination, but
it looked uncomfortably like Goody Gulde. The empty eyes
shone with hatred and accusation. Why did it persist in
staring at her?

She jumped back as the autumn wind stirred the limbs

of the puppets. The folds of her billowing cloak became caught in their carved hands, and she pulled them loose with unreasoning fear. The painted smile of the goodwife puppet seemed almost malevolent in its blandness.

What had she dreamed last night? There were the smells of the sea, but she could remember nothing more now. She did not want to remember the faceless thing that rose out of the depths, reaching for her with swollen hands....

Fiona turned away from the smiling puppet and shook her head in denial. Deirdre hesitantly touched her arm. "What's wrong?" she asked. "You look ill."

"It's nothing."

"Are you sure?"

"It's just me."

Deirdre wanted to make her laugh. "This one looks like you," she said, pointing to the freckled face and auburn hair of Gernie the Witchwife. "I knew you were an ogress!"

"I'm not!" Fiona shouted, unable to keep her voice from cracking with desperation. The blind eyes of the puppet were green pebbles flecked with gold paint. "How can you say that?"

Deirdre was startled by her vehemence. "I didn't mean to upset you," she said, the words drying up in her mouth. "I was only joking." She smiled unconvincingly. "You're much prettier than any puppet...." Her empty voice trailed away in the wind.

"What's this?" The two girls drew back as a man walked up to them, leading a bony horse. "You haven't been touching those puppets, have you?" he snapped, hitching up the horse. "They aren't toys for you to be playing with, so run along to your rag dolls! I can't be bothered with you now!"

He combed out his black hair with one gnarled hand, but his ill-humor faded as he looked at Fiona. The flecks of wan gold stirred in his disbelieving eyes.

"We haven't touched your puppets and we don't play with dolls!" Fiona said indignantly, temperment overcoming fear as she confronted the man. "Do you?"

He ignored her words and grasped the folds of her green cloak, examining the filigree of vines and leaves that caught the morning sun in silver. There could be no mistaking this pattern. "Gwyneth?" He whispered the name as if he had been struck in the belly, and his eyes widened with apprehension. The rede of the Old One...

Fiona pulled her cloak from his grasp and shouted, "You keep your hands to yourself!" Her face was livid and her own hands curled into fists. The surge of anger was comfortable and familiar as it gave her strength. Dead leaves cackled in the wind. "Who are you?" she persisted hotly. "What do you want?"

"Where is Gwyneth?" he demanded. "Tell me!"

"What are you babbling about?" retorted Fiona. "I don't know anyone called Gwyneth—!" She put one hand to her mouth as she remembered the ruined tapestry she had found in Harrow Hall. The face was now ravaged, but it was still that of the man rendered so lovingly in the tapestry.

"She has not even told you her name?" he said, frowning as he nervously rubbed the back of his neck. "Surely she has told you of the Mark!"

"Yes."

"Well, at least that's something," he said, drawing back to look at her with curious eyes. The lock of silver glinted in his coarse black hair. "What is your name?"

"What's yours?" she snapped.

"I call myself Greylock," he said, his voice edged with bitterness. He slapped the side of the wagon. "There, isn't it plain enough?" he asked, pointing to the faded letters of the name. His face was dull and vulnerable. He was pointing to more than mere letters. "Go on!" he yelled, clutching at the fragments of his past with gnarled fingers. "Read it for yourself! I was Greylock!"

Fiona stiffened, hearing only the hateful taunts she had endured in Balestone House. The ferns rippled out before her in billows that rose against the wind, and the morning tasted of burned cinnamon. There were sparks of hot gold shining in her braids.

The mouth of the goodwife puppet cracked open, and then the morning was broken by an agonized scream that filled them with horror. The painted features of the puppet rotted away as it screamed and pawed the air with swollen hands. Fiona was caught by its baleful gaze, unable to shut her eyes, and she felt her belly churning with bile.

Greylock struck the puppet to the ground and crushed it with a heavy rock, clutching his mouth as blood trickled from the squirming remnants, black with corruption.

"What have you done?" he whispered, grabbing Fiona by the shoulders. "It isn't enough that you've shed blood with your power! You must wave that foulness under our noses!"

"I—I didn't do it—!" Fiona cried, looking down at her trembling hands. "It's not my fault! I didn't know it would be like this—!"

She struggled in his frightened grasp, flinging out her hand to push him away, and tendrils of silver fire crackled as she touched him. He was smashed into the wagon, his garb in tatters over his raw, bloodied chest. The ferns were withered at her feet. He clumsily pulled himself up, blood streaming from his broken nose, and saw the fear in her wide eyes. "You don't even know what's happening, do you?" he said, snorting blood with each breath. "You must listen! This power that we bear must be set within wards

once it is kindled, or it will shrivel the mind with madness!
Do you hear me? It is already using you up!" He struggled
for breath. "Listen to me!"

Fiona looked up slowly. Dead leaves scuttled about her
feet, but she saw only horror in the gray eyes of her friend.
"Deirdre?" she asked, reaching out for reassurance. "Please
don't turn away now. It's still me—don't be afraid—" A
lump was congealing in her throat. "Please—?"

"Don't touch me!" Deirdre said, her voice cracking with
fear. "I thought you were my friend, not some awful—"
She clutched at her mouth. "Just don't touch me!"

"Please don't say that!" Fiona begged, hands clasped to
her breast. The dead leaves clung to her legs like withered
leeches. "I *am* your friend!"

"I told you so much about myself!" said Deirdre. "I've
never told anyone else, or trusted anyone else—! You aren't
my friend! You just pretended like all the others! I hoped
you were different, but you don't need me! You don't want
me to be your friend!" Her eyes were pale and lost. "I did
so much for you—!"

Fiona looked at the trembling girl in desperation. Her
freckled cheeks glistened with tears, and she suddenly
turned to run blindly across the fields of heather.

She did not hear her name called in the wind. Her eyes
reflected the lonely gulls, and she splashed through pools
of sweetwater, choking on the taste of mock honey. The
echoing cries of the gulls pursued her like ghosts. She was
too numb to feel the pain of the stones and branches in
her stumbling flight, although her feet were soon bloodied.
She could only feel the pain that ached within her breast.

She flung herself against the rusted iron bars and damp
ivy of the gates to Harrow Hall. Deirdre had said little that
made sense to her, but she understood the rejection in
those anguished words. What had she brought upon her-

self? She sank slowly to the ground and clutched the bars of the gate. Her head began to throb. Her limbs shook with chills.

"Fiona?"

She rubbed her puffy eyes. Dame Cracklecane stood over her, mantled in rabbit pelts and autumn leaves. Fiona looked up miserably, smoothing the folds of her kirtle with aimless hands. The woman bent to gently touch her face, blotched red with sobbing. Fiona longed for comfort but held back, her mouth trembling with determination. She must be strong.

"What is troubling you, my dear?"

"It's nothing," she muttered, wiping her runny nose on her sleeve. Why had she allowed herself to break down before Deirdre? "I—I hurt my feet on some sharp rocks," she said quickly, her head throbbing with icy pain. The woman frowned with concern. "I said it's nothing!" Fiona snapped, biting her lip as the pain grew worse. "Just leave me alone! I can take care of myself!" She forced down the bile that filled her throat. "Go away!"

"I hoped that you would trust me," Dame Cracklecane said sadly, opening her arms to the frightened girl. Fiona buried her face in the warmth of the rabbit pelts, struggling not to cry. "There, don't be afraid of your tears, my dear," said Dame Cracklecane. "Let them run freely, and tell me what has caused them."

Fiona told her what had happened at the stream, shaking with loss and disgust at her weakness. Dame Cracklecane grew pale as she described Greylock.

"Weland," she sighed, running one hand through her many braids. "He would come blundering along now." She smiled at Fiona. "I don't want you to worry over his words, my dear."

"But who is he?"

"He was once one of us, but he left the Mark," she said

quietly, pulling open the gates. "He killed his wife and his newborn daughter in a drunken rage, when he lost his mastery of the Fire. He has never rekindled it since that night, yet he torments himself by clinging to his old name of Greylock. The fool! But what can you expect of one who firmly believes that he was betrayed by The Lady?" She did not seem to feel the tears burning on her cheeks. The gate rattled angrily in her grasp. "You mustn't listen to any of his lies about The Lady! She offers mercy, and he will not accept it! He would rather blame Her for the ruin he has made of his life!" She bowed her head. "Why did you have to come back, Weland?"

Fiona did not answer, for she was suddenly doubled over with cramps that stabbed like ice, and her linen underclothes were drenched with sweat. The blood roared in her ears, and she clutched at Dame Cracklecane.

"I didn't realize you were so ill!" the woman gasped in dismay. "Let's get you out of this cold wind and into Harrow Hall!" She helped the sobbing girl down the cobblestones of the path, tenderly smoothing her brow, and brought her inside the main house. "You'll soon be fine, my dear."

Fiona grew less frightened as they walked down the long hall. The door to the obsidian chamber was already open, and its filigree of hawthorn leaves gleamed faintly in the amber sunlight that filled the air, warm and thick as honey. There were herbs upon the hearth that soothed her and made her drowsy.

Dame Cracklecane gave her fennel wine to drink, flecked with spices that drove the chills from her body. Fiona wrapped herself in one of the fleeces tossed upon the oaken benches. Slowly the bitter cramps faded, and all that remained was the dull throb in her head. She sipped more wine.

"Perhaps you would care to look at this tapestry," Dame

Cracklecane said, stirring up the coals on the hearth with an iron poker. "I've almost finished it."

The hearth blazed as redly as the sunset. Fiona stared at the rich, unfinished tapestry with wide eyes, for it depicted her clothed in the crimson and ginger finery of a queen, and she was crowned with silver. She stood in a field of flowers like clusters of gold bells, nestled in soft petals of white and saffron. The night above was emblazoned with huge stars.

"What are those flowers?" Fiona asked, breathing in the fragrance of cinnamon wood as she looked up at the tapestry. "I dreamed of them."

"Those beautiful flowers once mantled the quiet meadows of Therrilyn," answered Dame Cracklecane. She sat before her loom. "*Elithoe*, 'starbells,' they are named in the songs of the harpists, for there are none growing in this age of mills and muskets." She began to weave threads of gold and silver into the tapestry. "There is so little of that realm left to us, and few who remember it or the way of The Lady." Sorrow mingled with pride in her voice, and her fingers hesitated on the creaking loom. "I never wanted this choice to be forced upon either of us, my dear."

"What do you mean?"

Dame Cracklecane rubbed one hand across her eyes. "You have been blessed with great powers, which is to say that you have been chosen by The Lady," she said at last, raising her head with firm resolution. "I hoped you would come willingly into the Mark. I believe you would have, but we shall never know what might have been, not now. Weland has ruined all of that for us!"

Fiona struggled to open her eyes, feeling as if strands of sleep were brushing her face. The fleece was too heavy to lift from her shoulders. It was difficult to listen to Dame Cracklecane.

"Weland would not understand the many changes that

have given new purpose to the Mark," she continued, working on the tapestry with practiced grace. "There are new patterns that must be woven, patterns that follow the way of The Lady. You are needed to fulfill this intricate design, my dear."

The wide border of the tapestry began to shimmer as the quiet sunlight touched its hawthorn leaves woven of green and ginger, twining to form runes from its thick shadows. Fiona watched as the sun moved across the field of *elithoe*, burning like hazy gold, and the scent of cinnamon grew overwhelming, as if the flowers were real. And then she gasped in icy fear as she saw the dead leaves scattered among the flowers, with runes of web and soot that the sunlight did not dispel, black as veins of night.

Dame Cracklecane looked up in similar fear, for she had not woven the leaves. "I do what must be done for your sake, as well as for that of the Mark," she said, her brow shining with beads of silver mist. "You could not endure this rising of the Fire."

"What are you doing?" Fiona mumbled, forcing herself to her feet. She blinked at the goblet of wine in her hand, and abruptly flung it against the wall. The delicate strands of sleep could be seen in the air, glimmering from roof to walls in countless webs, and all were woven about her in trembling silver. The drowsiness was dashed from her eyes. She turned to run from the throbbing chamber.

"It is too late for you to flee," Dame Cracklecane said as she wove the final threads into the tapestry. "It was too late the very night of your birth, for none of us can escape the destiny willed for us by The Lady."

Fiona gazed at her and then stepped into the shimmering web of silver, only to clutch for breath as she was burned to the marrow. She stumbled to her knees, gnawing upon her lip as agony coursed through her like molten lead. The saltiness of blood filled her mouth.

"You need only yield to end the pain," Dame Crackle-cane said softly. "Fiona, spare yourself this needless suffering, for it is your own power that you fight. You cannot hope to overcome yourself." Her voice grew hard with guilt. "Do you enjoy suffering? You must yield!"

Fiona threw back her head, glimpsing bronze through her blurred eyes. It was the sword that she had found in the mud and reeds. She plunged into the fire and wrenched the sword from its place on the bench. The throbbing of her heart made it difficult to breathe, but she gripped the sword with both hands, staggering toward the loom.

Dame Cracklecane rose and stepped into the fire without harm. "I've no desire to see you suffer, but it is your doing now," she said, knocking the sword to the floor. "You might be my own daughter, but we are all daughters of The Lady. Her will has ordained that you must serve the Mark." She struck the struggling girl across the face as her composure fell into desperation. "Why can't you simply accept it? Why must you do this to me? Yield, you little fool! You will serve us, no matter how you struggle, for such is the will of The Lady!"

Fiona clawed at her white arms, drawing blood from the enraged woman, before slumping to the cold floor. She clung to Dame Cracklecane. The silver strands dissolved into the troubled air like dew.

"So it must be this way," Gwyneth murmured, bowing her head. "We've lost all that might have been ours. But there was no other choice, all because of Weland! He would never have understood our need—!" She closed her eyes, unable to look down at Fiona. "We should have been so close, sharing so much. Instead, you must be broken to our reins like a wild doe, no matter what the cost. And you will be broken, no matter how terribly you struggle, for your unskilled mind is no match for the power of the Mark." Gwyneth lifted the girl from the floor, cradling her in gentle arms. "And none of my shame or sorrow will ever win you back."

She angrily tossed her head. Weland was not the only one who opposed The Lady. He would not be long in summoning others to crush her dream. There was much to be done, for she did not mean to fail The Lady. The prophecies would all be fulfilled. They had to be! For there was nothing else that would still be hers after this day. She swallowed bile with her doubts. Fiona moaned softly in her arms, but she steeled herself to do what must be done now. It was for The Lady.

Six

DEIRDRE STOOD NUMBLY IN THE RISING WIND, leaves caught in her tangled hair, and looked out across the dark fields of rippling heather. Harrow Hall raised its towers behind the groves of apple trees and willows, the sun glinting coldly on bronze shutters, but she could no longer see Fiona.

"I've done it again," she said to no one, struggling to laugh at herself. She choked it back in despair. "I dreamed of having just one true friend like her, and when that dream happened..." Her voice grew brittle and obsessed. "I don't deserve her friendship. I shouldn't have done it, but I was just so scared—!"

"You had good reason to fear," Greylock said, coming up behind her. He gingerly wiped the blood from his nose. "You needn't fear me as well, lass."

"It wasn't even that," she said, talking past him as if she were alone in the world. "I was just so afraid of telling her! I could have told her about it, but she would have left me, the way they always do when they see through my smiles. But she left me anyway, didn't she?" Her eyes were still with bewilderment. "I didn't believe that she could do this to me. I wanted to help her...."

"She called you Deirdre?" He hesitantly touched her on the arm, disturbed by her thin voice. His worn fingers were light as a bird's bones on her sleeve. "I also want to help your friend."

Deirdre shook her head, as if noticing him for the first time. "I don't have any friends," she muttered, ignoring his hand on her arm. "Well, I don't need any, so I don't care if she never comes back. I don't care at all."

"You do care, but you would rather pity yourself." His instincts told him to assail her fears. "I know that feeling very well. It's so easy to blame everyone else for your own troubles, isn't it?" He shook her roughly. "Isn't it! Tell me the truth!"

"What do you want from me?" Deirdre shouted, pulling her arm from his grasp. Her face was pallid. "Do you want me to say that I'm weak? A coward? Well, I admit it! And I don't want to hear that it took courage to admit it, either! Fiona tried to tell me that, but it was a lie, just a lie, and both of us knew it!"

He chose his words with care now. "I'll wager that she didn't mean all that much to you, or you wouldn't have driven her away," he said, watching as her eyes widened. "What was she to you, Deirdre? Just someone to use when the loneliness was too bitter to endure, isn't that so?"

Deirdre blanched at his mocking voice and blindly swung her hand at him, only to have him clutch it by the wrist, his grip gentle but firm.

"Let go of me!" she shouted, struggling to pull herself loose, then kicking him in the shins. "How dare you say such things about me? She's my friend, the only true friend I've ever had, and I'd tell her so if I could! Dear Lady, why did I say those things to her? I'd give almost anything to take back my words! —Let go of me!"

"I didn't mean to hurt you, but it was the only way for me to learn your true feelings," Greylock said, releasing her wrist. Her gray eyes darted wildly, birdlike. "Deirdre, do you hear me at all?"

She looked down at the damp ferns. "It's all true, you know," she said at last, unable to look at him. "I'm ashamed of myself, but you were right about me, about everything. I was just so frightened!" She tried to smile. "I didn't know it was so plain to see. I always imagined that everyone was fooled by it." The quivering of her smile troubled Greylock. "I was only fooling myself."

"You needn't take my words to heart," he said, brushing back his tangled hair. "I was talking about myself. There's nothing wrong with you that growing up won't heal."

"Do you believe so?" she said intently. Her eyes caught his and demanded proof of his words. She slowly touched his weathered face. "Do you believe that our deepest wounds can be so easily healed?"

Greylock flinched at her touch. "You are too young for despair," he said, moved by an inexplicable fear. His daughter would have been no older than this haunting girl. "You must listen to me," he continued, gently taking her hand from his face. "Do you know where your friend has gone? I must find her, for she is in grave peril." He frowned at the decaying puppet in the ferns. "I fear she isn't the only one in such peril. I must find her!"

"She lives at Harrow Hall." Deirdre pointed across the fields of heather toward the ancient manor. "She's the ward of the Marl."

Greylock snorted blood from his craggy nose. "I hadn't anticipated that, but it fits with the rede of the Old One," he mused, rubbing his chin. "I've little notion of what has happened to the Mark. This surely demands their presence if my fears are more than nagging ghosts." He looked up at the drifting scarlies and shook his head. "I could be living in the Scathe," he said softly. "I didn't have to come back here, you know. No one asked me, or forced me; there wasn't any summons from the Mark. It was my choice." He sighed in chagrin. He was apologizing for his conscience now.

"What's all this about?" said Deirdre. She grimaced at the blood on his lined face and would not look at the rotting puppet. "What's wrong with Fiona?"

He weighed the consequences of telling her and realized that he must, for he could not reach the girl alone. "Do you know the legends of Therrilyn?"

"I grew up with them in the country, but we were taught not to believe in Balestone House," she replied, puzzled by his question. "What do legends have to do with Fiona?"

"Everything!" he said grimly, disturbed to hear how the old ways were being hastened to their death. "Fiona was born with the Mark of The Lady. She is heir to great powers, but she does not realize that those same powers are now consuming her life, burning it up like tinder. I must find her before she is destroyed by her gift." He gazed intently at Deirdre. "It may take her life, and it will surely take her mind. Do you want that to happen? It will, whether or not you believe in the legends. I don't even ask you to believe me. Simply believe in your feelings toward Fiona. I will need your help to save her, Deirdre."

Her gray eyes could not be fathomed. "I'll help you," she said at last, nervously picking the dead leaves from her kirtle. "I'm not sure what you expect of me...." She gave him an uneasy smile, but there were secrets in one corner of her mouth.

Greylock opened the wagon door and drew a patched brown mantle over his ragged garb. "I hope we won't need this," he said, reluctantly taking a sword from the wagon. "I haven't wielded it in years."

The ebony hilt glinted with twining vines and leaves of silver. He slowly drew the sword. Hawthorn leaves and eight stars were cut into the bronze of its blade. He regarded it with cold eyes and then sheathed it. The sight of it was icy water dashed in his face. He buckled it by his side, but he hoped to need nothing more than his hawthorn staff. He could not break his vow to Maeve.

The morning wind stung his eyes with brine, and he gave an encouraging smile to Deirdre. "I don't believe we'll have any trouble, unless it is with the Law," he said, locking up his wagon. "You're sure that you want to come with me?" She nodded firmly. "Then let's be on our way to Harrow Hall."

Deirdre followed him across the damp heather, clutching her thin cloak around her shoulders as the wind rose. It bit with teeth of frost. Gulls aimlessly blew like chaff in the weak blue sky. The smell of ripe apples mingled with that of sweetwater and wild mint. Dry leaves crunched beneath their feet. The cries of scarlies were brittle as icicles over the stillness that gathered upon the meadows, a stillness as intangible as the pale sunlight, but as real and intense as the pounding of the sea.

"Do you feel that?" said Greylock. "The very air burns with the Fire. There is something dreadfully wrong here, and it may be more than Fiona." He ran bony fingers through his hair in apprehension. "The bonds are weakening, and the many things that slept are now stirring under stone and root. It has been prophesied by oracles, but it was always supposed to happen in the years to come, never during our own lifetimes. Well, the years have come, and there is no putting it off for another day." He smiled wanly. "I may well be mistaken, of course. But my words often fell on deaf or disbelieving ears in Kelgardh. I insisted upon notions that were seldom liked by my kindred, who had grown far too enamored of the past. I left at last, but for reasons that had little to do with the Mark." His voice momentarily cracked. "You are very good at listening, Deirdre."

She modestly lowered her eyes. "I dreamed of going to Kelgardh," she said wistfully. "You say that you once taught there?" He nodded. "I taught myself how to read with some old hornbooks, even before school at Balestone House. I even wrote some songs. Just simple verses set to old tunes, but all my own words. I can do figures, too. Is that enough for me to go to Kelgardh?"

"It's more than enough," he said. "You seem to respect knowledge, unlike the numbwitted heirs of Nethernesse! Their fathers sent them there to learn, but they regarded anything more than hunting snow-apes and guzzling ale to be worthless! It had to be endured, for their families have always guarded the lands of Kelgardh. And there is always one who craves to learn all that is in the world. That is a rare pleasure."

He grew more serious. "I believe that you could easily earn one of the eight chairs in the Scholary," he said. "You needn't spend more than a half-year in the Common School. I might be able to put in a good word for you, if my word still has any worth in Kelgardh." He laughed curtly. "Never mind about that! You'll get where you're going, Deirdre."

They went on through the fields of heather. Billows of brown and russet leaves parted before them, only to scratch at their heels. The rusted iron gates rose up to bar them from Harrow Hall.

"Now what?" asked Deirdre. "Shouldn't there be a bell, or something?" She hugged her waist tightly and looked about with subdued eyes. Bronze shutters glinted from the towers. "The gates are locked, aren't they?"

Greylock drew an iron key from his belt. "I've had to use this during lean years," he grinned, working the key into the massive lock. "I'm certainly no master thief, but this seems simple enough." He nodded toward the green shutters of the main house. "You keep one eye peeled for servants. We don't want to be clapped into gaol. I can assure you that it is no pleasant sojourn."

Deirdre stepped back and clasped her hands. "I should be brewing tea for the headmistress now," she murmured. "I'm sure to get a birching for this." Her eyes darted about in fear and excitement. "You said that it seemed simple enough! Hurry!"

Hooves clattered loudly at their backs. "Well, what's this?" inquired Lethan. He sat easily in his saddle, but one hand rested on the oaken stock of his pistol. "Perhaps you can tell me what you are doing here? I'm not used to finding thieves at work in broad daylight. You're either very bold or very thick. I'm willing to hear your words before packing you off to the House of Magistrates." The sun glinted from his spectacles, but his eyes were not hard. "There's work to be found in the workhouses, if you are penniless. Why must you descend to thievery?"

Deirdre could not help but giggle at his earnest voice despite her fear. Greylock stepped between her and the mouth of the pistol. "We are not thieves," he said firmly. "You must listen to me, Lord Harrow."

"Why is that?"

"I must speak with your ward, for she is in such peril that each moment brings her closer to madness or death," said Greylock. "I am sure that you would not want her to suffer the fate of your sister. So if you will only allow us to see her—"

"What's to stop me from shooting you down where you now stand?" But he lowered the pistol and looked thoughtfully at Greylock. "What about my ward?"

"Fiona bears the Mark of The Lady," said Greylock. "Do you know what that means? Your parents may have spoken of it to you, Lord Harrow." He met the startled eyes of the young Marl. "I knew them very well, but this is hardly the hour to speak of it. Fiona is my concern now. You must realize the nature of her peril!"

Lethan shook his head. "Gwyn promised me that it would never come to that," he said softly, speaking more to himself then Greylock. But doubt lingered in his voice. "I seem to recognize you, fellow. What is your name?"

His words were lost in the shattering roar of stone and thunder from Harrow Hall. The highest tower was crumbling in sheets of silver fire, and molten gold poured from the walls like marrow from cracked bones. Willows were uprooted as the earth buckled, and their green leaves boiled in the scalding air. The iron gates snapped from their hinges, clattering on the worn cobblestones.

Lethan fought to calm his rearing horse, its white eyes rolling wildly, but he could not calm himself. His eyes were those of the terrified boy who had seen his world torn apart by the very forces that now raged before him. The years were stripped away with inexorable brutality.

"No!" he shouted in desperation. The reins whipped out of his cold fingers, but he did not feel it. "I won't let it happen again!"

The blast of thunder tore him from the saddle. Deirdre was flung to the ground beside him, while hot ash choked their every breath. They rolled away from the trampling hooves of the frightened horse. Greylock clung to his staff. Blistered leaves spattered like hot grease across his face, but he did not look away. He watched as the tower fell into ruin, molten gold bubbling from its gnarled roots. He realized that what had been set in motion could not be halted. Yet he refused to abandon all hope.

Deirdre slowly rose to her feet, clutching the folds of her thin cloak. Her face was smeared with ash and sweat, but fear did not dim her eyes. She saw the pistol in the singed heather and hid it in the pocket of her cloak. The wind from the sea began to dispel the floating ash, and she licked her lips for the tang of brine. The taste of it gave her renewed strength.

She squinted her eyes. "Dear Lady," she murmured. The remains of the tower jutted through ashes and steam, jagged as a broken tooth. Who could live through that?

Lethan struggled to one knee. He was bruised, but the

soft earth had saved him from broken bones. He found
that his spectacles had been crushed by his runaway horse.
The gray blur across the lawn of pea grass was the tower
his father had reclaimed from the encroaching wood. Now
it was shattered. Everything was shattered.

Deirdre saw his dazed eyes and helped him up. "Lean
on my arm," she said, looking for Greylock. "What's happened to Fiona? She isn't—?"

"I am quite sure that she is unharmed," Greylock replied
as the ground lurched once more. "Lord Harrow, did you
speak of Gwyneth?" The nobleman jerkily nodded his head.
"I never imagined that she would go this far, but it makes
frightening sense now." He gingerly touched the welts on
his face. "You are close to her, Lord Harrow?"

"I thought so...." Lethan looked down at his crushed
spectacles and saw fragments of his ashen face. "You belong to the Mark?"

"Once, but not for many years," said Greylock. "I know
that you have little reason to trust me, but you must believe
that this land is in peril of destruction. There are powers
awakening that will not yield to your Law." He glanced
about in haste. "Your home will soon be swarming with
gawkers and soldiers. We must hurry if we are to catch
Gwyneth!"

"How do you know her?"

"She is my sister," Greylock said reluctantly. It only
clouded the matter now, but that could not be helped. "I
put little hope in the fact. She is more likely to heed you."

He began walking toward the ruined tower. Bits of leaf
blew in the sea wind, glistening with beads of gold. Deirdre
and Lethan followed after him, exchanging puzzled glances
as they failed to recognize each other now. The taste of
spring grass and wild thyme stirred beneath that of ash,
refreshing as cold lime tea. Greylock feared it, even as it
invigorated him. The memories it invoked were more

tempting than he had imagined. It was only the realization of what it truly meant that enabled him to resist that temptation.

There was also the vow he had taken for Maeve. But he did not want to be reminded of it now, not with so many other reminders of the past confronting him. He gripped the bole of his staff with determination.

"What's all this about?" Lethan muttered, still leaning upon Deirdre. His legs felt like reeds. "Gwyn never told me of her brother, if she even has one." He attempted to laugh and choked on it. "I really know very little about her. She simply came into my life and filled it. I never knew it was so empty until I met her...." His low voice trailed off as he remembered Deirdre. "I shouldn't worry about Fiona. She seems quite capable of taking care of herself. Or so she has impressed me—" He frowned. "What is your name?"

"Deirdre," she told him shortly. The air thickened with ash as the remnants of the tower loomed before them. "Do you feel a prickling just under your skin? I still don't know what is going on, for all this talk of some mysterious Fire." She angrily tossed her dirty hair. "I'm just concerned about Fiona. That's all."

"We'll find her," said Greylock. He did not dwell upon how she would be found, but he had an unpleasant notion. The nape of his neck was frozen. "Just don't be frightened."

"Where is she?" said Deirdre. She stared at the blocks of obsidian, still oozing steam and molten gold. "How could she have lived through this destruction?"

Greylock pointed into the billows of hot ash. "There," he said, waiting as two shadows moved toward them. "I feared it would be this way."

The shadows became Fiona and Gwyneth. Each was clad in kirtles of royal crimson, red as crushed berries, and mantles of star-gold that smoldered with the pungence of raw ginger. Crowns of silver wrought as hawthorn leaves and twining vines were on their heads, with braids of silver woven among their own braids. They stood like mother and daughter, even to the beads of mist that burned pale silver on their brows. Fiona moved with the stiffness of a puppet, and her eyes lacked any glint of awareness or will. Gwyneth was behind her, bearing a folded tapestry over one arm, head raised in glory.

"Weland, what have the years done to you?" she murmured at last. There was pain in her soft voice. "You should have remained in the Scathe."

"I would have been content to do just that," he replied curtly. "But events have an uncomfortable way of pulling one back into the world. I heard tales of blood offerings. The scattered bits of rumor hinted at worse things. I remembered the prophecies and came back to delve into them." He rubbed the back of his neck. "I didn't imagine that you could go to such lengths, Gwyneth."

"I do what must be done to fulfill the prophecies," she said, throwing her head back proudly. "What can come from it but good? The old ways are dying and will soon be forgotten if nothing is done! Do you want this land to be set drifting into darkness? It will be only that, for all talk these days of knowledge!" Lethan stared at her with bleak eyes, but she could not look at him. "Weland, don't you understand at all? I love The Lady! I would be nothing without Her!"

"You would probably be the horse trainer you dreamed of being before the Mark," he said gently. "Do you remember how you made up your own names for the horses? They answered to those names, Gwyn." He shook his head. "You would have made something of yourself even without The Lady."

Gwyneth forced herself to be harsh. "You've grown soft

and cloying over the years," she said, struggling to restrain unexpected tears. "What has become of the warrior who went into the depths of Pel Lendwrei? You gloried in doing battle with the spawn of Witcherie!"

"I'm no longer that simple boy off the farm," he said as pain creased his face. "Nor are you the wide-eyed little girl who ran off that rainy night to follow Thyri. We've grown up since then, Gwyn. There are too many years between us and our youth."

"Is that so?" She frowned, her brow dripping with sweat as well as beads of the Fire. "I feel as if those years have been sloughed away! The gift shines within me like the very stars!"

"It's not yours," he said angrily. "You're leeching it from this child!" He swept his staff before him. "Just look at this ruin! She must have struggled horribly against your bonds to wreak such destruction. How can you justify this in the name of The Lady?"

"I wanted it to be different," she insisted. "It would have been if you hadn't blundered into things. She would have willingly entered the Mark." Her eyes glinted with passion. "We have need of the power she bears, for we would fulfill the prophecies of The Lady!"

"How, Gwyn?"

"I would open the tombs of Mymmorë. I would awaken the sleeping Queen of Therrilyn. I would serve her gladly as she sweeps away this gray world of mills and workhouses to renew the way of The Lady." Sparks of hot gold burned in her black hair. "You know the legend of the last Queen. The prophecy was that she would arise after long centuries and restore the might of her people. It is in the nature of prophecies that nothing may stay their fulfillment. Ygerna shall awaken, and the splendor of the past shall be reborn." She held out her hands. "There is no need for us to be enemies now," she said hopefully. "Join me, Weland."

"I cannot," Weland answered, raising his hawthorn staff before him. "How worthy is your dream if it depends on using an innocent to fulfill it? I hoped to turn my back upon the Mark. I wanted nothing more to do with it." He swallowed as he stepped toward her. "I cannot turn my back upon this, my sister."

Gwyneth drew back softly. "Ah, no," she whispered, her eyes flickering with loss. "Please, do not force this choice upon me, Weland. I don't want to see you hurt any more, but not even you will stop me, my brother." Beads of pale silver gathered upon her brow. "What of your vow to Maeve?"

"You shouldn't have spoken of that," he said coldly. A hardness touched his eyes, concealing the memories stirred up by her words. "I will stop you, Gwyn!"

She wearily nodded her head, as if all the strength had gone out of her, and then looked up stiffly. "You bring this upon yourself!" she cried, reaching out to grasp the bole of his staff. Her eyes were as bleak as a leafless branch. "It is your choice!"

Weland straightened his back as her fingers touched the black hawthorn. The bolt of pain struck him with the fury of summer lightning. He struggled for an agonizing moment, and then fell writhing to the ground in defeat. Ash clung to his face. Bile churned deep in his belly. He had not been able to break his vow. He would not summon the Fire. He felt the hilt of his sword digging into his ribs, but he knew that he would not unsheath it. He could not fight Gwyneth. He could not do anything.

Gwyneth sighed and dropped the staff. "Weland, is this what you wanted? You are my brother, but that will not save you from worse than this, not if you persist in fighting the Mark." The sparks of hot gold smoldered in her hair. "They will surely kill you then."

Weland slowly rose to one knee, his face gray with more

than ash. His staff lay on the blackened earth. Droplets of gold shone like dew on its gnarled haft. He looked at Gwyneth. It had been too many years now. The words of concern were for their memories of each other, and of themselves. They were strangers. The children they had been were ghosts. All that remained was to become enemies.

Lethan could no longer keep silent. "Jennet?" he said, struggling for his words. "I know that we made no pledges to bind us, but what we shared—" His voice was vulnerable and raw. He clumsily held out his hands. The slipping reins had bloodied them. He did not feel that pain. "Did you lie all along?" he asked. Everything had slipped from his hands. "I have to know!"

Gwyneth bowed her head. "What we shared is gone," she whispered in anguish. "It's all my doing, so you had better forget me." She gazed achingly at him. "Please, my dearest!"

Deirdre carefully drew the forgotten pistol from within her cloak. She had heard enough of their sorrowful words and regrets. None of it would help Fiona. Mere words never did help. She knew that from hateful experience. Her stepfather had taught her that much.

She raised the pistol with both hands and pointed it at Gwyneth. "I don't want to hear you talk," she said. "I just want you to let go of Fiona." Her eyes were cold. "Now! I won't tell you again, you witchwife!"

Gwyneth smiled with disdain, but her mouth grew taut as she realized that the girl was serious. The hammer was drawn back upon the pistol. "Put that down," she said, struggling to remain calm. "Do you truly care for Fiona? Then you will kill her if you shoot me now."

"You're lying!"

Weland held out his hand. "She isn't lying, Deirdre," he said hoarsely. "They are bound, and if you kill one, then you will surely kill both." He stepped toward Deirdre. "I know that you want to help her, but there's nothing we can do now." He was appalled by the jealous need that surged dark and wild in her eyes, driven up from depths that he dared not plumb. "Give me the pistol, Deirdre."

"We can't just let her go!" she persisted. "There must be something you can do, just *something*—!" She reluctantly lowered the flintlock. "I didn't mean those terrible things about you, Fiona..."

Weland reached out and quickly took the pistol from her hand. "I can't stop you here, but this is not the end of it, Gwyn," he said firmly. "Do what you will. For now."

"I'll do what must be done," she said, walking into the shadows of the forest. Withered leaves swirled about her and Fiona. The lingering mists gathered behind them, shimmering with wisps of silver fire, and the morning wind brushed their footprints from the ashen ground.

Weland watched them go, his weathered face creased with resignation. There were no choices left to him. Gwyneth had chosen for him. He would also do what must be done, even if he lacked her faith. Necessity would serve just as well. It was all he could depend upon now.

He gave the unwanted pistol to Lethan. "You had better attend to your home, Lord Harrow," he suggested, wrapping his dirty cloak around his shoulders. He wiped the lank strands of hair from his brow. "I'd like to poke about in this wrack for a while, if you don't mind."

"Yes," said the recovering Marl. "Yes, do whatever you must"—he sheathed the pistol—"Weland, isn't it? Yes, of course...." The glint of curiosity enlivened his eyes. "We must talk when all of this is over, friend Weland. I'd like to know of your acquaintance with my parents. I'd like to know of many things. But that must wait for now. There's more that needs attending to than my home."

Lethan hesitantly touched his false lock of silver. It might still bring him luck. So much of his life seemed to be just as false. He abruptly turned away from the wreckage of the tower. He could not dwell upon that now. There was much to be done. Anything, now.

Deirdre stood in the singed grass while scarlies cried out hungrily in the wind. "You simply let her walk away from us," she accused Weland. The wind listlessly plucked at her matted hair. "How could you do that?"

"I couldn't do much else," Weland replied curtly. "You almost got us swatted down like three flies, brandishing that pistol!" He jabbed at the cinders with his staff. "What do you expect of me? I can't whistle up the winds, or make gold out of cow dung, or change my skin. I never could, not even in the old days! None of us can do such things!" He snorted with bitter laughter and his eyes were grim. "That may all change, for the prophecies seem to be coming true. —Now, will you help me look through this ruin?"

"I want to know what you're going to do," Deirdre said, stubbornly folding her arms. "What's in all of this wreckage that could possibly help Fiona?"

"I'll know when it's found!" he retorted, rubbing the nape of his neck. "But we won't find anything at all if you don't stop chattering! Get to work!"

"Well, you don't have to snap at me like some crotchety old tortoise," she muttered, kicking at the heaps of cinders. "Do you really expect me to sort through all of this—" She stopped, catching her breath. "Oh my..."

Silver glinted among the ashes. Deirdre knelt down and brushed away the shards of obsidian, still hot with veins of gold. A cattle goad of blackening silver lay on the ground. This was surely an offering of luck or The Lady!

"Here, is this what you wanted?" she said, holding out the cattle goad to Weland. "Fiona used to carry it with her like a talisman."

Weland turned the goad in his hand. "Where did she

get this?" he asked intently, shaking his head at the pattern of twining vines and hawthorn leaves. It must be luck, and not The Lady!

"Oh, she's always had it," Deirdre said brightly. "She once said that it's been in her family for years and years." Her face grew puzzled. "Do you mean that it's important? I thought it was just an heirloom."

"It *is* an heirloom," he said, his knuckles white as he clutched the dull goad. This was more than he had wanted to find. He felt the weight of prophecies in his hand. "It's been in her family for years and years, has it? I shouldn't be surprised...." He laughed uneasily, handing the goad to Deirdre. "You'd better hold onto this for Fiona. It's very old, and no doubt precious to her. I'd hope for reasons of her own," he added grimly, thrusting his staff into the warm ashes. Sparks flew up, swirling in the wind. "But there's no use brooding over that now."

"I don't know what you're talking about," Deirdre said as she dropped the goad in her pocket. "No, don't bother to tell me, since we don't have time for chattering, as you've said already." She smiled coldly, barely revealing the tips of her teeth. "What do we do now?"

"Now we must speak with the Marl of Ciaran," he replied uncomfortably. He took a deep breath, but the taste of brine in the wind did little to fortify him. "Well, are you going to stand there like a goosy girl? Come along!"

Lethan watched the flames leap up the walls of his home as he waited for Egil. The servants were hurling buckets of water in an effort to contain the fire, and it appeared that they would save most of the main house. But the ten warning bells still rang out loudly along the roof, just as they had that night, long ago. He heard lingering echoes of the past even when the bells ceased to toll.

The branches of willows shivered about him as the wind blew, and his face was dappled with the trembling shadows of narrow leaves. He adjusted the spectacles he had taken out of the scholary. At least some things were easily replaced. The rest would be more difficult.

A crowd of gawkers had gathered at the gates, but these were held back firmly by servants and Scathlings. He did not want his home looted while he was gone. He refused to dwell upon the notion that he might not come back. Egil would ride with him. He would come back.

"Hoy!" Egil came striding through the willows, leading two horses by their knotted reins. "These brutes should suit us, Lord Harrow!"

Lethan nodded, watching as billows of smoke poured from the windows of Harrow Hall. The life he had known was swept away in that smoke, scattered by the wind. He swallowed the bile and grief that had filled his mouth. There was nothing else he could do now.

"They'll save most of th' main house," Egil said, going up to the brooding Marl. The horses snorted uneasily, and he rubbed their shaggy manes. "Ye'll have it looking as it did afore long."

"I suppose so."

"Supposing is for th' numbwitted!" Egil snapped. "Ye'd not be mooning over that lying trull, would ye? She betrayed ye, Lord Harrow!"

Lethan swallowed once more, his gray eyes blurring with anguish. "I won't have you speaking of her that way," he said softly, his voice catching like a rusty lock. "I don't know how she could have—" He stopped, clenching his fists. "Just let her go, Egil."

"Ye'd best be doing that yourself, then," Egil muttered as he mounted his waiting stallion. "I'll not be speaking of her again, if that's the way of it." He frowned, raking his

fingers through his loose hair, deftly winding it into a knot
at the nape of his neck. "Just set your mind t'other things
if ye've any wits."

Lethan mounted his own stallion. "It's over, and there
isn't any use bemoaning it," he said, grateful for those cold
words of comfort. "You've always been here to lean on,
like a good, strong oak. I've need of your strength once
more, if we're to help Fiona."

Egil slowly rubbed his chin. "Aye, even if it fetches us
into th' Witchwood." His brow grew pale beneath its alder
leaves of woad. "Ye needn't be blaming yourself for all her
troubles, Lord Harrow."

"I'm responsible for that girl, and all that happens to
her will be on my head." Lethan clutched the reins, ignoring the pain of his bloodied hands. "I've mucked up
things from the beginning, Egil. It's just as well my father
isn't alive to witness it." He straightened in the saddle, and
his eyes were troubled. "But since he isn't alive, we'll do
things my way!"

"Ye couldn't know that it would be coming to all this,"
Egil protested, dismay in his leathery face. "I'd not be so
hasty to enter th' depths of th' Witchwood! Do ye say that
it shelters n'more than legends?" His brow was furrowed
with memories of dark tales, although he would never
forsake the determined Marl. "Why should ye be th' one
to set things aright?"

Lethan nudged his spectacles to the bridge of his thin
nose. "I've got to, old friend." He clasped the southron by
his brawny shoulder, and then urged his stallion toward
the Witchwood.

Seven

THE PATH WAS NARROW, with tendrils of moss hanging from the gnarled and fragrant pines, and patches of moonlight shivered in the rustling leaves. Fiona felt herself walking through the forest, although she had no choice in the matter, and her strained features were carved of icy marble freckled with brown gold. Yet there was furious awareness deep in her unblinking eyes, and beads of sweat trickled slowly down her face as she struggled against the unseen bonds that enchained her within the shell of her own body. She resisted the warm haze that gathered in her mind, tempting her to surrender and sleep, spinning soft, misty webs so enticing that she had to fight her own desire to yield.

Dame Cracklecane walked beside her, the tapestry on one arm, following the moonlit path as if she had walked this way many times. There were dry leaves in her braids, still dark red and even tinged with fading green, from the branches that plucked at her along the path. Her rich mantle of star-gold was streaked with wet moss, but it seemed that the forest had anointed her, rather than smearing her garb. There was even some moss on her cheek which she would not wipe away and seemed to bear with solemn joy.

The earth was soft beneath their feet, and the damp air tasted of loam and dead leaves slowly decaying into darkness over long years. The wind in the branches murmured of water and root and time, woven through the soil in an intricate web that held crumbling bones and transformed them into new life in patient silence, until green shoots emerged from the black earth out of death. There was an unceasing rhythm here that even Fiona sensed through her anger, a wellspring of holiness that seemed quiet only because it was present in all things, yet so strong that it could not be bound or subdued but must be accepted as one accepts existence itself. The rhythms of sun and seasons, blood and birth, sea and stone were woven in the one changing, changeless rhythm of being by the hand and the heart of The Lady.

All this Fiona sensed dimly, and she understood that it was not greed or hatred that moved Dame Cracklecane, but love for the green, growing world of The Lady.

Now the billows of gold and white mist that unfurled in the darkness burned more brightly than she had ever seen before, and countless newborn stars blazed fiercely in the night. The antlered moon rose above the stars, sweeping the oldest before it like amber and ashes, while its lonely white glow bathed the crown of the forest in cold, dreaming light. The leaves seemed to throb with it, and Fiona knew it for the throbbing of her own heart.

"Here is the womb of The Lady, from which this world is continually born and sustained," said Dame Cracklecane as the path darkened before them, splattered with moonlight and the dry shadows of countless leaves. "Here you can feel the deep strength of existence that has been buried beneath the mills and the workhouses and the Law. Here is the ancient power of the earth, slumbering beneath the calm, ordered world of men for an age, but preparing to emerge into the sun once again." She turned to look at Fiona. "I wish we had not been driven to this bondage, but when you have learned why we needed your power so desperately, before you were even ready to offer it freely, perhaps you will find it within your heart to forgive us, my dear."

Fiona winced inwardly at the appellation, and she would
have screamed if she could just move her tongue; but her
only possible reaction came in tears of rage that burned
down her cheeks. How could she have allowed herself to
trust and even hesitantly love this woman?

The path began to widen, and she saw the yellow glow
of lanterns through the thick branches, floating like the
ghosts of fallen stars among leaves and beards of moss.
There were massive earthworks rising against the moon,
crowned with dark oaks and thorns, too entangled for
swords or torches to tear down, and too daunting to be
climbed; old bones and ring-mail were caught in the huge
thorns, covered with moss and pallid web, and antiquated
helms of crumbling bronze lay heaped with skulls within
at the bottom of the earthworks. The lanterns of star-gold
and isinglass burned over huge gates set within the earthworks. The gates were made of black wood and mossy
bronze, gleaming with silver filigree of hawthorn leaves
and a wreath of stars. There were three lanterns, which
must have been burning for untold centuries with none to
attend to them.

The leaves rustled loudly over the path as a falcon flew
through the branches, scattering strands of moss, and came
to rest upon the shoulder of Dame Cracklecane, its talons
biting into her flesh. It was creamy white, with flecks of
brown on its breast, and its wide eyes were bits of frozen
sky.

"Gos, where is your master?" she murmured, stroking
the soft white plumage of its head, wiping the moss from
the iron hook of its beak. "Go and fetch him!"

The falcon uncurled its cruel gray talons and soared up
through the branches, through the frail lace of shadows,
into the leaf-edged moonlight. Dame Cracklecane saw the
drops of fresh blood fall from its talons, and she rubbed
her shoulder with uneasy fingers. The falcon cried out

coldly as it flew into the nothingness that existed under the seething ocean of stars and milky gold that filled heaven. She watched it fly across the night in silence, her heart beating with its white wings, and then she looked at the blood on her fingers, warm despite the coldness of the autumn wind. She closed her hand but clasped nothing, unless it was her own life. Perhaps it was enough, even now.

"More than enough nonsense!" she muttered, rubbing her hand clean on her kirtle, both shamed and angry with herself for no discernible reason. "Helskarth is near, and soon—" She forced herself to look at Fiona. "Soon we shall see, my dear."

The stillness of the night was broken by the wailing of a hunter's horn, harsh as the presage of winter that rode the edge of the wind, overtaking its own echoes as it approached the gates. It was answered by the icy cry of the falcon, all but its voice lost in the night sky, and iron hooves drummed in the depths of the forest.

"They come!"

Fiona groaned inwardly, and she renewed her struggle to cut the unseen web that bound her, spinning ever more tightly about her with soft, inexorable threads.

The forest seemed to open in a flurry of leaves and wet moss, scattering icy moonlight across their faces, and riders appeared through the low branches. Each wore mail of bronze and silver rings, glinting beneath the folds of green mantles filigreed with gold vines, and ebony-hilted swords of bronze hung at their sides; each wore an ivory mask worked with pale gold runes, and carved with the same proud, arrogant visage; each wore their hair in loose braids, those of the men tipped with amber and onyx, those of the women tipped with raw bone and hawthorn leaves wrought of silver.

They parted as another came riding out of the forest in

grim splendor, his shaggy white mantle sewn from the pelts of snow-apes, his headdress the hide and antlers of an enormous stag. His left arm was bare, the sinewy flesh white with deep scars, and his garb was the dark crimson jerkin and breeches of a hunter, including the sheepskin boots and pouch of herbs strapped to his left leg. He wore no mask, but his face was always in shadow, save for the glint of his gray eyes. There was an old hunting horn at his hip, along with a sword whose hilt was a writhing serpent of ebony and silver, clasping a moonstone in its coils. One hand was never far from that sword, which was sheathed in antique goldenwood.

"So this is the child, eh?" he said softly, gazing down from his huge black stallion at Fiona. "We have been waiting for you, child. We have waited for an age."

Fiona glared angrily at him, but this irruption of grim and savage power from the slumbering depths of the forest had frightened her more than she dared to admit to herself. Legend had risen up from the dark places of the earth. She chose to watch the white falcon as it plummeted down to rest upon the arm of the antlered horseman.

She realized that he did not bear the Mark. He did not possess the power that she shared with those who had gathered here: her unwanted kindred. But there was a merciless core of iron will in him that seemed more threatening to her than the awakening power that burned in the night. The power he bore was brutal and cold.

"The hour has come," he said, stroking the wings of the restless falcon with lean, lazy fingers. "She must now open the gates of Mymmorë."

"Let it be done," said Dame Cracklecane. Her voice was warm with the deep satisfaction of one whose unwavering faith has been affirmed after years of loneliness. She gently set one hand upon Fiona. A swirling veil of silver fire enfolded them. The air tasted of sage and red mallow.

Fiona felt herself pressing both hands against the hard black wood of the gates, and the filigree of hawthorn leaves ran with silver at her touch. She could sense the entwining webs of power that bound the huge gates, rooted in the earth that upheld them.

The shimmering pattern of leaves began to throb beneath her hands, throbbing with the beat of her heart and the slow throbbing of the countless stars: and it was all one primal, holy rhythm which had nothing to do with the designs of those who clustered in anticipation at her back.

Dame Cracklecane clasped her shoulder more tightly, and the fingers sank into her numb flesh, weighing upon her bones like talons of ice and smoldering lead. The riders began to chant hollowly within their ivory masks, and Fiona could feel their gathering wills in her mind, unleashing the wellspring of unknown, unknowable power that was her birthright, and the madness that was its consuming shadow. Brown leaves blew in the rising wind, but the runes set upon them were now written in drops of blood, and she felt that she could read them, as if their secret language was hers alone to know.

She began to sense the intricate windings of power that bound not only the gates, but what lay beyond them, slumbering for centuries of night and stars and purpose. She seemed to glimpse with her mind's eye the golden domes and black towers of an ancient city, with fountains of hewn stone and quiet groves of goldenwood...and then she saw the shroud of moss and leaves that now covered Mymmorë. Yet, although the city was empty and silent, it was not dead. She sensed the presence of a dreaming will, powerful even within the dream, waiting for one to awaken it.

The night was slowly gathering into an immense anvil of darkness shot through with unbound stars, raining threads of milky fire and raw gold across the Witchwood. A sudden wind gusted out of the basalt crags of the Westering, tinged with scents of rare herbs and early frost, rustling with flurries of dead leaves. The fixed stars were pale as candles in the shuddering night.

Fiona felt her mind screaming as it was clutched by the combined wills of the Mark. The huge gates began to tremble as her awakening power flowed through them, and the knots of sorcery were severed like bits of string. She seemed to see the ancient webs that bound the gates unravel under her cold hands, wisping like smoke...and her mind began to unravel at the same time, drifting into the witless dark....

The jagged ruins of white stone that towered above the villages of Sorl splintered the moon and flung its glistening shards into the sea. The graceful shadows of whales darkened the waters, plowing the depths without knowledge or need of the designs of men.

The moving stars were clustered together over the edge of the ruins, swimming in billows of white and gold mist, and slow trails of ginger and silver and cinnamon were scrawled behind them. The forgotten kings hewn from the cliffs seemed to hold the massive ruins up to the night.

An unbound star that shone white and bitter gold roared out of the heavens, cleaving the autumn sky with huge slashes of saffron. Thunder rumbled in its long wake like the blast of countless cannons, scattering the pungence of cloves as it plunged into the waiting cliffs.

The night reverberated with the echoes of the fall, and the sea rolled back in swirls of creamy froth, only to return and batter the cliffs in churning blows. The brooding kings shaped from the cliffs stumbled, and worn slabs of stone were sheared away in slow, grinding moments that crushed the work of centuries. The foaming beaches were strewn with shattered limbs. The fallen star smoldered fitfully among the wreckage of the kings of Sorl.

The villages below huddled in the silence of cedars and

willows, but that silence was broken by the bellowing of
conches from the ruins, where none dared walk at night.

Elspeth sat before an unfinished canvas that depicted a
hall of oak and gray stone that had caught fire, with a
vague figure walking through the flames. She painted in
the clear moonlight, her face touched by the shadows of
the bars in the window. The quiet glints of gold were almost
drowned in her deep green eyes.

She abruptly stiffened as the window began to rattle in
the wind. The walls oozed with drops of molten gold, and
the air was crisp with the smells of crushed thyme and
splashing water and summer thunder. The tip of her brush
shone like an ember and burst into flames that spread
across the canvas in moments.

Elspeth rose from the hard oaken chair and walked to
the door. It was locked, but as she set her hand upon its
bronze latch, beads of silver fire glistened on her brow like
sweat. The door exploded outward in shards of black oak
and spatters of molten gold.

She closed her eyes with the torment of bitter memories
that had been locked away for ten years. There was still
much that was clouded, but she remembered enough to
fill her eyes with rage as she went down the hall, leaving
ashes and silence in her wake.

Remerie loomed in cliffs of old, weathered basalt above
the rolling waves of the sea, far to the east, where no ships
had ventured save in legend. There was no life on that isle
of barren stone, save for the kelp and pale, golden jellyfish
that were dashed against its gnarled cliffs and clung to the
spurs of obsidian that were its bones; within its encircling,
unbroken walls there were only meadows of gray ash and
ruins sprawled on dead earth.

The lonely murmur of the sea was drowned in the thunder of a falling star. It burned with the green-gold fire of summer as it pierced the few tatters of sea cloud, drawing beads of mist down with it like warm seed, until it buried itself deep within the core of Remerie.

The warmth of the fallen star slowly began to flow into the dark, bleak stone of the island, kindling the ashes of an undying power at its heart. It sent forth tendrils like the budding shoots of spring.

The old woman threw dried herbs and twigs of alder into the coals, her bony hand set upon the ugly lump of basalt that had stood in the clearing for untold years. She had come to this place since early childhood, when she had been taught the old ways by her grandmother, and she in turn had taught them to her own granddaughter. Much good it had done! Caitlin was lost to the House of Haldir. Who would pass on the old ways now?

Yet she herself could not understand the meaning of the runes she had fashioned of the hawthorn kindling, nor that of the strange words she had spoken over the black stone. Much had been forgotten through the Age of the Axe. Perhaps there was no wisdom or power left in the old ways. Who still gave true fealty to The Lady?

She threw the last of the twigs into the fire, looking at the stars that blazed above the Witchwood. How many would fall this night? She had hopes of finding handfuls of gold strewn in her garden. It would be quite pleasant to live out the remainder of her days in comfort.

All thought was scattered by the agonizing bolt of pain that pierced her hand, but she could not pull it away from the black stone, not even when her blood flowed down the runnels carved for that purpose: and then it was too late to scream as her eyes went dark.

* * *

The Mountain of Kings was mantled in the unmelting snow of forgotten winters, but in the quiet woods and valleys far below, autumn still reigned in dark red and faded gold, with deep wells of shadow untouched by the moon, and skins of ice forming over clear streams.

The lanterns of small villages flickered at the edge of the pine and maple forests of Nethernesse. Each had its bell tower and row of sugaring vats guarded by tall hedgerows of hawthorn; each had bonfires crackling in the fields of lonely farms, throwing gnarled shadows on their oak and white stone walls; and each had raised its Brown Man.

Hollow logs filled with hot, glowing embers marked the long flanks of the Mountain of Kings. There tribes of bears and snow-apes dwelled above the deep valleys, their caverns sweet with pine boughs.

The autumn night shuddered as a huge star blazed downward in red flames, glowing as if plucked from a forge. Clouds of golden haze burned in its wake, and with thundering fury it struck the snowbound crags of the Mountain of Kings.

Billows of snow filled the night, obscuring the face of the mountain, and roaring winds stripped the crown of the forest in a swath of dead leaves. Bands of fur trappers watched in awe from their rough camps along the slopes of the winding valleys, clutching both their muskets and wealstones in tight fists. The wind skirling off the mountain tasted of wild thyme and cinnamon.

The fallen star melted its way into the depths hewn for it in another age, while a pall of mist and ashes formed over the Mountain of Kings.

Fiona saw the massive gates opening before her, and she could sense the webs that had bound them stretching across the length and breadth of the world. She had touched fire to an immense pattern of power, as if an ember had been flung into a pool of oil, and there was no quenching it. She could sense the knitting of bones and the congealing of metals deep within the crucible of the earth; she could sense the whispering of the dead, and the twining of roots, and the murmuring of years like ghosts.

The opening of the gates startled the combined wills of the Mark. Their hold slipped like loose reins. Fiona could feel the power within her welling up without restraint. She grasped it with her own furious will, ignoring the pain that throbbed in the nape of her neck, struggling to tear the web that bound her within her body. Each heartbeat was a hammer against her breast, but she felt her cold hands curling into fists, and she bit deep into her lip, tasting the warm blood in angry triumph. Dame Cracklecane screamed as the tapestry on her arm burst into flames.

Fiona crumpled to her knees, gasping for breath, as the fire that consumed the golden tapestry seemed to burn through her limbs. She dimly glimpsed the woman stumbling back into the darkness of the wood, and she felt loss through the anger that sustained her strength.

Helskarth drew his sword, its black iron blade glinting with runes of pale gold, and shouted, "Catch her, fools! She mustn't escape us now!"

She felt rough hands clasp her arms, and she was pulled to her feet. She glared up at the antlered horseman with defiant eyes; blood trickled down her chin, and despite the weakness that drained her, she struggled to wrench her arms loose from the hands that clutched them.

Helskarth gazed down at her, his face still hidden by shadows. The antlers of his headdress glistened icily in the moonlight. The white falcon preened itself, perching upon his scarred arm, regarding her with cruel, unblinking eyes of frost. Helskarth raised her chin with the tip of his sword. Fiona looked up at him with raw hatred.

"I did not dream that your power was so great," he said softly, amusement in his voice. "Yet that is all the greater reason that it serve the Mark." The falcon clashed its gray beak, and he fed it a gobbet of meat from the pouch that hung at his saddle. "We feed upon power as this winged one feeds upon flesh."

"There is no need for this!" said Dame Cracklecane. Her eyes flashed angrily as she pushed the sword away from Fiona. She lowered her head. "We have used betrayal for the sake of The Lady. This must shame us, no matter how urgent and noble the need. We must not revel in that shame with arrogance and needless cruelty." Her voice trembled with severity. "It is need for The Lady! Not the tainted needs of men for gold and chains and thrones! We must never sink to such depths!" She proudly raised her head. "We do what we must for the love of The Lady."

She turned to Fiona. "I know that you do not understand all of this now," she said gently. "I only ask that you find it within yourself to forgive what we have done, for we never sought to hurt you, Fiona."

"I ask no forgiveness," Helskarth said, raising his iron sword so that it hung between them. "I doubt she is inclined to offer it, eh?"

Fiona ignored the mockery and spat at Dame Cracklecane. "What do you want me to understand?" she said coldly. "Your lies? Your play at friendship? I must have made you laugh, clinging to your skirts for comfort, you lying sow!"

"You can't believe that!"

"Why should you even care about it?" Fiona shouted, her eyes brimming with unwanted tears. "I trusted you, almost as if you were my own mother, and you—" She swallowed before her voice could crack. "You've got what you wanted, so spare me all of your kindness! I don't want it! I don't want any of your lies! I don't want anything from you!"

She sought to lash out with the hatred that was burning within her, but it twisted into blinding pain as she summoned up the Fire. She felt as if jagged ice had pierced the nape of her neck and shattered into thousands of barbs. "No!" she cried in agony. "Stop it!"

Dame Cracklecane reached out and touched her brow with gentle fingers. "You must stop it," said the woman. "There is nothing else you can do now."

Fiona yanked her head away in revulsion. "Don't touch me!" she gasped, warmth spreading through her numb body. "I wish you were dead!"

Helskarth chuckled. "It must be galling to possess the power to fulfill your wish and yet be unable to wield it," he said as she sagged in the grasping hands of the Mark. "Wish away! It will do us no harm." The falcon on his arm clashed its beak as if in agreement, and he fed it another gobbet of flesh, his long fingers smeared with blood. "You shall serve our wishes before long, child."

"No!"

He laughed once more, but it was lost in the roaring of a flintlock pistol. Blood gushed from the mouth of his dying horse as it crumpled under him, and he was flung to the hard ground. The white falcon soared into the night.

Fiona pulled herself loose from the startled hands that grasped at her. She barely had the strength to stand on her shaking legs, but she had to run before her captors could hold her back. Helskarth was pinned beneath the bulk of his slain stallion, but in moments he lifted the carcass over his head and flung it aside with disdainful ease. Fiona realized that he was more perilous than all the Mark. There was in his eyes such emptiness that she could not meet his cold gaze, and she turned to run.

"Fiona?"

She felt her heart jump at the sudden voice and turned to face it with small clenched fists, her kirtle swirling about her like smoke. Dame Cracklecane stood before her, features weary in the moonlight, holding out her hands to Fiona. The shadows of rustling leaves dappled her arms, but pale silver mist clung to her hands like ice and sweat. There was still a smear of moss on her cheek, and her tired eyes were dimmed with sadness. Fiona slowly looked at her and murmured, "Why did you do this to me?"

Dame Cracklecane said nothing, although her throat grew taut with unspoken words of regret. Fiona cried: "I trusted you!"

The cry unleashed all the grief and hatred that churned within her breast. A rage of leaves came sweeping out of the darkness, wailing in the fierce wind that was her own cry of overwhelming anguish. Dame Cracklecane covered her ears with horror. Fiona barely heard the screaming of horses as blood rained down from the night. It burned her face like blinding tears.

Hot ash mingled with the blood on her face, and through the pain that misted her eyes, she numbly saw an unbound star falling from the heavens. Its trail smoldered in ginger and silver as it plunged across the face of the moon, and she saw that it was falling toward Mymmorë.

The surge of thunder tossed her through the ashen night as the star buried itself in the hidden ruins. The forest was spattered with drops of gold as white and ginger mist poured over the massive earthworks, blazing with hot flecks of silver and crumbling sparks. Fiona struggled weakly to sit up, her nostrils swimming with blood, her head pounding as if it would burst. The trees around her had been smashed into kindling, and many more were wreathed in flames. The charred air reeked of blood and burning, while huge cracks veined the flanks of the earthworks, oozing with molten gold. Fiona climbed to her feet, appalled by such devastation.

She felt gentle hands on her shoulders, and she quickly turned her head to see the brown, weathered face of Egil the Scathling. "Ye needn't be a-fearing me, lass." She lowered her fist, brushing the mess of blood and ashes from her numb eyes. "Come along, aye?"

Dame Cracklecane appeared out of the mists that burned through the wounded forest. "Yes," she urged. "Go with him while there is time, my dear." The night rang with enraged shouts, and she unwillingly looked back. "I never wanted it to be this way."

Fiona searched her tired face, smeared with ash and age, through which her eyes shone like pieces of the sea, gold and green, shimmering, stirring in their depths, filled with old dreams that had risen like the faceless bodies of the drowned to haunt her sleep. Fiona heard her words, and heard within them words she could not speak for all her sorrow. Fiona did not know whether she could bear to hear those words, much as she longed for them. She only knew that she was confused and lost and hurt.

"I thought you cared for me," she persisted, hanging on the burly arm of the Scathling. "You let me care for you and even—" She could not say the word, but still reached out to the quiet woman. "Why did you have to lie?"

"Egil, take her back."

"Please!"

"It's no use talking," said Dame Cracklecane. "There's nothing more we can say, nothing—" She quickly turned her head away as her throat quavered. "Hurry! Go with Egil!"

Fiona looked at her and realized at last that there was no longer any woman called Dame Cracklecane. There was only the stranger called Gwyneth. Fiona had never known her, and she watched helplessly as the woman walked into the swirling mists, insubstantial as all ghosts.

"Lass, come along!" Egil muttered, drawing her into the deep rustling shadows of the forest, where horses waited for them in a hollow of ferns and reeds. The dappling moonlight was steeped in golden haze, while unconcerned stars burned in the distant night. She welcomed the harsh cries of scarlies tearing the stillness that choked the heavens.

Lethan stood by one of the horses, the flintlock pistol clutched in one hand, his face scratched by brambles and cold with fear. The false lock of silver shone congealed beneath his ear, an icy lump that no longer protected him against the darkness, and his eyes seemed to cower behind the spectacles he wore, frail as the remnants of his world. He had not been spared that destruction.

"Ye'd have done well to shoot that horned demon, rather than his wretched horse!" Egil roared, mounting his steed and reaching down to Fiona. "Grab hold, lass!" She grasped his arm and was lifted into the saddle. "Well and done! I won't let ye fall," he added, grinning. "Lord Harrow?"

The shaken nobleman looked up and nodded grimly. "We'd best be on our way, no matter what is left to us," he said as he mounted his own stallion. He still clasped the flintlock pistol, but he seemed almost startled to find it in his hand. "Who knows what else is happening to this world?" He looked back at the smoldering haze that crowned Mymmorë. "Gwyneth," he murmured, giving her up to the night. There was too much that demanded his presence of mind for him to grieve now. He must be the Marl of Harrow.

The harsh wail of a hunting horn mingled with the cries of scarlies drifting between the shimmering web of stars and the blackness of the Witchwood. Fiona heard it and clutched the gnarled arm about her waist in fear and exhaustion. Egil drew his sword, black even in the moonlight, chanting a warsong as he raised the iron blade and invoked the names of his ancestors.

Riders burst through the underbrush in a flurry of dead leaves, their ivory masks glistening with spatters of cooling gold, blotting out the runes of paler gold. Silver fire ran along their bronze swords, pulsing with their heartbeats, and the antlered moon seemed to ride before them, lighting their path through the trees.

Egil gripped the reins of his stallion in his teeth and turned in the saddle so that his body shielded Fiona, even as the first rider galloped toward him. A trail of silver fire burned through the night, but Egil spurred his horse forward, plunging beneath the sweep of the bronze sword— and then his sword chopped through mail, crunching bones, scattering rings of bronze and silver in hot, gushing blood. The silver fire faded as the rider cried out and toppled from his horse, dead before he struck the ground. Egil shook his sword clean and tugged on the reins, turning his stallion to confront another foe, his eyes gleaming with satisfaction.

Fiona gazed at the dead rider, whose blood still poured from the brutal wound in his side, and she felt her belly churning with bile. The memory of her father butchering pigs for the winter filled her mind, vivid and dreadful, but she could not escape it.

She looked away at last and saw another rider galloping toward Lethan. Her sword blazed with silver fire, her braids flailed down her shoulders. "Lord Harrow!" Egil bellowed as she swung her sword back to slash at Lethan, who watched with pale eyes, the pistol shaking in his hand. The bronze sword floated in the night, light as a moth's wing, shimmering with the fire that sustained the stars. Lethan slowly raised the pistol and fired it. He realized at that same moment what he had done.

The rider was smashed out of the saddle by the force of the pistol ball, her ivory mask and the face beneath shattered into ruin. Wisps of silver fire still clung to her sword as it fell to the ground. Lethan watched as her body crumpled in the ferns. He could not look away despite his revulsion.

The remaining riders held back, their horses tearing at the ground with worn hooves, frightened by the acrid scent of gunpowder. Lethan shook his head. The faceless body looked up at him.

The riders still hesitated across the hollow, for it was plain that none had ever seen gunpowder fired, but they would not let that restrain them for long. The hunting horn called through the black forest, and their swords blazed up with the Fire.

"Lord Harrow!" cried Egil, galloping up to the nobleman and clasping his shoulder. "Ye mustn't fling aside your wits now!"

"I know—"

Lethan swallowed with effort and thrust the pistol into its sheath, turning his horse toward the quiet meadows beyond the forest. The riders suddenly spurred their horses across the hollow, trampling the bodies of their slain kindred, even as the white falcon soared before them on the rising wind.

"'Tis our hearts they'll be wanting now, and there's no mistaking it!" said Egil. "Hold tight, lass!" He urged his stallion after Lethan.

Fiona clung to his arm as he galloped down the winding path. Tendrils of wet moss spattered her face, dead branches tore at her mantle. The warm folds of star-gold snapped about her, and hooves drummed angrily, but all that she heard was the pounding of her heart.

The horse stumbled over twining roots of oak. Although it did not fall, she was flung from the saddle into the thick underbrush of reeds. Egil called out to her, turning in the path, but her head throbbed too much to answer him. The pale stars seemed to blow away like leaves, and her eyes trembled shut.

Gwyneth stirred the burning rags of the tapestry with a branch. Sparks of silver leaped up, but all that would remain was a heap of ashes, waiting to be scattered to the wind. A pang caught in her throat. So much had come to ashes.... But it was useless to dwell on that now. She must sacrifice her own longings for the sake of The Lady. Just as she had always done.

"Enough!" she cried furiously, stabbing the branch into the ground. Enough of this whining like some witless child! It was weakness, and she would not indulge in it. "I won't—!"

Gwyneth turned away from the tapestry, startled by the crunching of dead leaves and twigs. She tore the branch from the soft earth, its tip still smoldering like an ember, and beads of silver crawled on her brow. The air tasted of ginger with each slow breath.

Helskarth came striding through the mist, blood and wet blotches of moss on his shaggy mantle of snow-ape pelts. The massive headdress still concealed his face with shadows that clung like spiderwebs. His gray eyes glinted icily from that emptiness as if chipped from stone, and there was no pity in them.

"You let the child slip out of our grasp," he said, and momentarily raised his sword. "Well, no matter! We'll catch her soon enough." The runes of his sword quivered with life in the ragged moonlight. The pungence of ginger mingled with that of moldering leaves, sour and black. "I'll set my pack upon her trail; power is easily sniffed out, and they'll have no difficulty in catching *that* scent!" He grinned. Gwyneth could not see it, but she knew that he grinned.

She felt its coldness like the slash of a whip. "She may well be a match for them. I'll not scoff at her power, having seen it!" His voice rang like iron. "But she'll be no match for our numbwitted friend out of the Haugh. —And there's no need to scowl at me, my ally! It may be distasteful, but we'll do what we must for the Mark."

"It's distasteful to me, at least." Her face was drawn in coarse lines, and she did not lower the smoldering branch. "You've grown to savor that foulness, and not merely for the sake of the Mark."

"What does it matter, so long as the prophecies are all fulfilled? You were willing enough to lend your power to that foulness, as you've so nobly scorned it!" He quickly tossed his head, as if scenting blood on the wind. Leaves rustled in the sweep of his antlers, scything the mists. "I don't need you flaunting your conscience under my nose! It's a bit late for that, isn't it?"

Gwyneth flinched at his sneering words, unable to deny them. "I know," she murmured at last. "It's too late for so many things...." She struggled to find the fervor that had sustained her over the years, but all that remained of it was duty. "We are allies, even if we're no longer friends. It should be enough to see us through this night. We're so near the end of our labors! Ygerna is waiting to take the reins of power from our hands—"

"It won't be that way," Helskarth said, his fingers closing into a knuckled fist. The white falcon came to rest upon his hand as if clutching an oaken stump in its talons. Drops of blood trickled down his arm. "Ygerna will serve us well, but the reins of power are knotted fast in *my* hands. There's no other way for the Mark."

"You would betray even The Lady?" Gwyneth demanded, raising the branch as if to strike him. Sparks of gold burned in her tangled hair, and the dry leaves falling about her glimmered with the faintest breath of the Fire.

"I could happily fling your powdered bones to the wind—!"

"Perhaps you could, even now." Mist swirled about his antlers in slow tatters, making his voice tangible with each harsh word. "But you won't have the chance, my dear. —*Hai*, Gos!"

Gwyneth cried out as the white falcon flung itself into her face with slashing talons. It splintered the branch with a snap of its beak, and tore the flinders from her hand. She was momentarily blinded by the furious whipping of its wings; then blood spattered from her mouth as a merciless blow sent her sprawling to the ground. Helskarth knelt by her side and clutched her throat, his fingers squeezing the breath out of her.

"Now, listen to me," he said, digging one knee into her ribs. "I still have some use for you, although you've turned cloying and soft. Be still! I'll gladly leave you here for the crows if you struggle, my witless ally! There are others who would eagerly take your place in the Mark."

Gwyneth tried to turn her head, the emptiness within her worse than the brutal pain inflicted by Helskarth. Dear Lady, how could this be happening now? "No, no, no..."

His fingers tightened about her throat. "You've little to say, unless you choose to serve the Mark. There's much to be done!" he whispered urgently, forcing her head back. "We must gather in our strays, whether or not they wish it. That is simple enough, isn't it? Isn't it! And those who refuse to serve us must be killed, mustn't they?" Gwyneth shuddered helplessly, bled of her strength. "But you won't have to be killed, because you will serve us, my dear. You will! There is nothing left for you but the Mark. That's so, isn't it?" His knee sank deeper into her side, and his eyes glittered in the swirling mist. "Tell me now!"

Gwyneth nodded, for there was nothing else she could do now. The lies and betrayals had been gnawing away at her for years. No matter that it had always been for the Mark. She was worn down to the nub. This was all that she deserved. A sob of anguish caught in her throat. Nothing was left. She had not only failed herself, she had failed The Lady.

Eight

FIONA SAT UP SLOWLY, and dead leaves crackled under her legs. The moon seemed to be fluttering from branch to branch like a huge moth. She rubbed her eyes, grimacing at the hot stab of pain that swam in her head. The screeching of an owl dashed all thoughts of sleep. She was lost in the depths of the Witchwood.

Moonlight glinted patchily in a tiny pond fringed with yellow reeds and hollyhock. She gently washed the grime from her face, listening for the clatter of hooves, but there was only the creaking of branches in the wind. A handful of mint leaves served to dry her fingers, as well as cover up the smell and stickiness of fear. Scarlies cried out hungrily in the distance, and she bit down on her lip. She had not felt so alone since the loss of her family.

Dry branches scratched at the moon as she carefully got to her feet. A lump of ice throbbed painfully at the nape of her neck. She pulled her mantle about her shoulders, aching and cold.

The deliberate rustling of leaves startled her, and she clenched her fists. Sweat trickled stingingly on the scrapes she had gotten this night. Fear buzzed inside of her like a trapped bee. It seemed as if the trees were closing in about her, blotting out the moonlight.

A long match sputtered in the darkness. "Fiona?" asked the girl who stepped into the glade of hollyhock. "I've been looking for you the longest time!" The match threw off thin curls of sparks. "You had better come with me, or else we'll both get caught."

She smiled, and her plain features glinted with dots of gold, carefully freckled upon her cheeks. Her brown hair had been cropped and looked more like a drover's cap. She wore an old-fashioned kirtle of red velveteen, buttoned to the hollow of her throat with ivory pegs; gold buckles gleamed from her shoes, which were ugly and black. She might have stepped out of an illuminated hornbook.

Fiona folded her arms. "You haven't even given me your name, and you expect me to follow you through the woods?" she snapped. "I'll do no such thing!"

"Tansy is my name, and they're not going to change it," the girl replied, holding up the match. "I don't need any of their overstuffed titles! You won't find a fancy bone in my body, and that's how I like it." She frowned at Fiona. "I'd never wear such finery, not even to court."

Fiona ran her fingers over the rich folds of her mantle and bit her lip. "I didn't choose to wear it," she muttered, angrily reminded of Dame Cracklecane. "Anyway, it's none of your concern!"

"No, it isn't," Tansy said uneasily, glancing about the glade of hollyhock. "You *must* come with me, or you'll never get away from the Mark! They won't accommodate you by dying as easily as Goody Gulde!"

"I don't know what you mean!" Fiona tossed her aching head in desperation. "She slipped, and that's all! Deirdre told me, so just leave me alone!"

Tansy stared at her with bewildered green eyes, flecked with gold. "You're one of them!" Fiona gasped, feeling all the strength drain out of her limbs. The leaves rustled with silver fire...

...and she opened her eyes to find that she was in a warm bed, wrapped in a green and yellow quilt. The air was heavy with the fragrance of steamed herbs. Deirdre sat beside her in a goodwife's chair.

Fiona attempted to sit up among the soft pillows, but a splintering pain shot through her head. She gingerly settled back into the pillows. Deirdre raised a mug of hot milk and sweetwater to her dry lips. Fiona sipped at it, allowing the dollop of mock honey to soothe the rawness of her throat. A touch of drowsiness eased the pain of her poulticed brow, but she wanted to stay awake, and so she placed the mug upon the table by her bed.

"That should make you feel better," said Deirdre. "You shouldn't move about, at least not yet. You look as pale as a pot of boiled leeks, with freckles." She laughed, but her eyes were concerned, and lack of sleep was smeared like soot beneath them. "Do you know that you've been fast asleep for three days now?"

Fiona looked about the dim room as her eyes adjusted to the solitary glow of a whaling lamp, which reflected the black oak walls in its curving glass chimney. A rack of harpoons hung upon one wall, their iron barbs glistening with tallow, their black ash hafts bound in hard thongs of bear sinew. A large sea-chest sat beneath the shuttered windows, its bronze bands and cumbersome lock encrusted with verdigris, decorated with inlay of scrimshawed whalebone. She heard the slow, constant crashing of the ocean, and the air tasted of brine even with the windows shut tight, their diamond panes trembling despite the protection of stout shutters. An unceasing wind rattled across the shingled roof.

"Where are we?"

Deirdre slowly stretched her arms, wincing as her bones seemed to crack. "We're in Ciaran Hall," she yawned, rubbing her shoulders and the back of her neck. "I've a room all to myself, with servants!" She tossed her amber hair, which fell softly down the green velvet of her jacket and loose breeches. "Do you like my new clothes? I've lots more, all the gift of the Marl. She'll want to speak with you later, but you may rest for now." She yawned once more. "I've been keeping everyone away from this room, especially that Donal." She managed to turn up her nose while blushing with affected modesty. "He's the son of the Marl," she added quickly, gathering her hands in her lap. "He's always making cow-eyes at me, and fetching sweetmeats for me, and pestering me to walk along the cliffs with him." She lowered her voice. "But no one is allowed to go walking after sunset," she said. "I never imagined there were so many soldiers in the Three Towns! The country is all flooded with fear, and not even daily hangings are enough to stop it!" The glittering in her gray eyes was that of sparks leaping up from heaps of ashes, excited and wild. "There is even talk of war!"

She stood up, rubbing the small of her back. "I wasn't supposed to talk about that now," she apologized, tucking the heavy quilt about Fiona. "There, how's that? I want you to rest." She smiled wearily. "I could do with three nights of sleep myself, to be truthful." There was something harsh in her voice, as if she were mocking herself. Disgust showed in the tightening of her mouth, but she wiped it away on her sleeve, and then smiled once more. Her pale eyes shone wetly in the glow of the whaling lamp. "Why are you looking at me that way?"

"How long have you been sitting up with me?" Fiona said haltingly. Her tongue felt dry and swollen. "You didn't sit in that chair for three days, did you?"

"I've been here for as long as you needed me," answered Deirdre. She flinched as the wind tore out shingles from the roof, her eyes suddenly vulnerable and lost. "I just wanted to do something for you," she said softly. "I didn't mean to say those awful things. I was just so scared—!"

She bowed her head uncomfortably, turning away from the bed. "I've got to tell you something, but it's difficult." The cords of her throat were strained, and she abruptly closed her eyes as if struggling to calm herself. "I can't talk about it now," she said at last, forcing open her eyes. "It's not so simple for me to put into words. It's never been simple for me. I wish things were different—I want to be different—"

The longing in her low voice was avaricious, and as she turned, her eyes shone fiercely in the yellow lamplight. She sought to turn with the indifferent grace of the Gentry. It only made her look foolish.

Fiona lowered her eyes in embarrassment. "It was good of you to sit up with me," she murmured, gathering her sheets into lumps with nervous hands. "Your new clothes look very nice."

Deirdre clasped her own hands behind her neck. "Do you need anything?" she asked, stirring up imagined dust with the toe of one slipper. "No? I could get something—" A wan smile creased her mouth. It might have been angrily drawn in chalk. She loathed it. But she only said, "I'll be back in a while."

Fiona sat up, floundering in the pillows, but the older girl hurried from the room. Shadows rippled from the dancing flame of the whaling lamp, soft and dark. The air was still brittle once the shadows had settled to the floor. Fiona did not know what either of them should have said...something to cut through their cocoons. Why was it so difficult to simply talk?

The shutters banged furiously in the wind. She pulled the quilt up to her chin, but the nape of her neck still felt cold, tingling as if stung by mild hornets. It seemed that her senses were both heightened and numb. She plumped up the pillows and eased her shoulders into them. The wind loudly tore out another row of shingles from the roof.

She recalled childhood tales of wind-walkers and gaunts, which had always frightened her late at night. Perhaps such things were more than mere tales now.

Fiona did not want to think about that. She hesitantly touched the herb poultice upon her aching brow and found that her hair was gathered within a linen bonnet such as children wore when they were ill. She angrily pulled it off and flung it upon the floor. She was no child, not after all that she had endured, and she would not be treated as one! She combed out her hair with quick jabs of her fingers. Her brow began to throb like a drum, but she did not stop until her hair was spread in auburn heaps on the pillows. She smiled with cold satisfaction. It was foolish, but it also made her feel less helpless. Her cheeks burned with utter humiliation and rage at the hateful memories of being used, but she could not wipe those memories from her mind. It brought up bile. She made herself swallow the lump in her throat. The memories churned deep in her belly. She could only swear that it would never happen again—never!

The bonnet lay mocking on the floor, crumpled and white as a lump of old snow. It was everything that she loathed in her life. It was meant to make her feel swaddled and small. Everything was meant to make her feel that way. She abruptly climbed out of bed, walking on tiptoe across the cold floor. Her brow ached horribly, but she gritted her teeth and forced herself to ignore it.

The sea-chest under the windows was heaped with her few belongings. Someone must have fetched them from Harrow Hall. She quickly pulled the patched farm garb over her fine linen bedclothes, tucking the legs of her breeches into the tops of her wading boots. The shutters rattled in the wind, and she decided to put on her floppy cap of rabbit fur, even as soggy leaves spattered against the bared windows. An immense moon rode above the storm, which was breaking up in huge mountains of cloud, black as anvils. She glimpsed the comforting beam from the lighthouse of Eádnarr.

There was something else on the sea-chest. She touched the bundle of cloth, hesitantly unfolding it. A bronze sword shone in the moonlight, its long blade cut with alder leaves and an antlered moon. She grinned. This sword, in the house of Morwenna Brightflower!

The grin slowly faded as she wondered who had unearthed the sword. It should have been buried deep in the rubble of the tower at Harrow Hall. Someone had gone to great lengths for an antiquated weapon. Bronze was little use in this age of steel and gunpowder.

"Oh no," she whispered, her hands trembling with the sudden realization. The sword burned coldly under the moon. "No!" Dame Cracklecane had said it: "Bronze in hands such as ours will prevail against iron and witch-spawn." And here was the sword, waiting to be taken in her hands. Why else would she be in Ciaran Hall?

Father was right, she fumed. I should have listened to him. Gentry always want something. She gave an angry snort of laughter. The Fire of The Lady! That was all they cared about, for all their fine words. They had never cared about her, Fiona. She was just an ignorant country girl. She had no beauty, no family, no home. She tried to believe that it did not matter, but it did, and she could not deny it. What else should she have expected of them?

She looked down at the sword. It had been cleaned, and the filigree of alder leaves ran with moonlight, cold as the waters of an early thaw. The blade was strong, forged to be wielded in battle. Yet it was finely wrought, more than was needful in a weapon. The veins of each leaf had been worked with delicacy and rich shadings that trembled like flakes of rust. How could its beauty be the work of the oafish People of the Stallion Banner?

The sword beckoned to her, and she felt an inexplicable pang of determination. She grasped the hilt. It belongs to me! She raised it with both hands. I found it, an offering of luck or The Lady!

The country saying struck her numb. Her father used it lightly, but her mother once told her that it belonged to the ways of The Lady. She had gotten her only birching when she used it in a coarse jest. Fiona had never seen her mother so enraged. The birching had drawn blood. The memory ran like an ugly crack through her childhood.

Dame Cracklecane had known her name that night. She had known her favorite lullaby...and it was her mother who used to sing her to sleep. It was her mother who remembered the ways of The Lady. It was all her mother's fault! Fiona tossed her aching head. What a lot of rubbish! She only had herself to blame for trusting Dame Crack-lecane. It was all too painfully her own fault.

Fiona saw her face running down the diamond panes of the window. The shadows of wet leaves blew across her eyes in the moonlight. She could not go on this way. She was tormenting herself, and it did no good. Why dwell on the past? It could not be changed. It no longer existed. Yet the empty face in the window accused her like a ghost. She closed her eyes, but the lingering face became that of Goody Gulde.

"No!" She was not to blame for Goody Gulde. It was an accident. And she deserved it. Everyone had loathed her, not just Fiona. And it was merely an accident.

She tightened her grasp on the sword. Everything was so confused! Rain mottled her reflection. She suddenly wanted to smash the windows, the walls, the moon that shone heartlessly down from the wrack of night. Every-thing—! But she knew that it was useless, and lowered the sword. She laughed mockingly at herself. It was already smashed into fragments. Everything in the world.

Fiona wearily bowed her head. She had to get away, but where could she go now? There was no sanctuary from all that had happened to her since that night. The memories had been burned into her as deeply as a debtor's brand. But she could not go on living so close to them—and it had nothing to do with Goody Gulde!

The sword grew heavier in her hands. She looked at the blade, pointing in her mind to the plains of yellow grass and the salt dunes of the southland. Who in that sunlit country would know of the Mark?

The notion attracted her like a lodestone, and she felt very pleased with herself. There would be no need to live in dread. Her life could be as open as the sprawling plains of that mapless land. She would have her own farm, and orchards of fruit trees, and dozens of hired hands. She let slip the reins of her fancy, watching from an immense porch as the sun drowned in seas of endless grain, her feet propped up on the railing, lazy as the sunset.

She sighed, for all of that would require the wealth of the Gentry. It would be helpful if a falling star blazed out of the night. —But one had fallen! She had gone to claim it and met Dame Cracklecane. It was hers! Dame Cracklecane had even acknowledged her claim to it. Now it would be wergild for all that she had endured since that night.

Lethan had carted it away, and no doubt was hoarding it under Harrow Hall. She angrily turned up her nose. That was just like the Gentry!

He owed her more than fallen gold, but she would settle for that now. Father always said that the wealthy respected nothing but wealth. She was entitled to her portion of that gold, and she intended to have it. Father would be proud of her determination. For once the country would take from the town. It was only just.

She bundled up the sword in its wrappings of muddy red velvet, tied it with her scarf, and slung it loosely over

her shoulder. The wettest leaves clung to the windows; the
rain dwindled, each drop promising to be the last; moonlight shone across the drenched meadows, glistening from
countless pools like so many pearls. She could easily make
her way to Harrow Hall.

The whaling lamp flickered at her back. She waited for
the door to open, then realized that it was only the dregs
of whale oil burning up. The starving tongue of flame
guttered out the next moment. Shadows hissed into its
absence even as she involuntarily held her breath. She did
not unclench her teeth until the darkened room accepted
the moonlight blurring through the windows.

What if the door had been locked? That fear struck her
like an axe, and it was all she could do to cross the room
in unhurried steps, forcing calm upon herself. But the film
of sweat that gathered on her brow felt like frost. She put
one hand to the bronze knob and slowly opened the door.

There was the quiet glow of crumbling embers at the
end of the dim hall. She could see the head of an antique
spiral staircase, gleaming darkly of oiled hardwood and
fittings of ruddy brass. The scent of pine boughs mingled
with the smoke from the downstairs hearth. The murmur
of voices drifted up the staircase, vague and wordless. There
were only doors and darkness at the other end of the hall.
Light whispered from beneath one of the doors. She gently
closed her own door and stepped into the hall.

Panels of maple were set within the stone walls, carved
with legends. Here was Birle of Wynder, battling the
gnarled People of the Root. Her legs were entangled in
the roots of alders, but her hounds surged among the foe,
and in her hands was the great sword Nemorë. Here was
Bain Lackwit, fiddling for his supper in the courts of Pel
Lendwrei. His fiddle was inlaid with runes, and in his eyes
waited the horror that he would summon from the depths,
wreaking his vengeance upon the heartless consort of

Ygerna. Here was Ishaunse the Mariner, setting sail for
the fabled isle of Remerie. Her face was to the rising sun,
but five whitherings flew before the prow of her ship,
foretelling that she would never return to the Hall of Ciaran.
Here were all the legends of this land.

Fiona walked down the hall, clutching the bundled sword
to her thin ribs. The voices grew clearer with each furtive
step toward the staircase. She stopped, peering through
the bars of the railing, and recognized the Marl of Ciaran.

Morwenna stood before the hearth, stirring up the coals
with a bronze poker. "This should drive away the chill,"
she said, putting another log on the fire. "Do you believe
that she will help us?"

The weathered man standing before the black windows
was the puppeteer, Greylock. "I don't know." He wearily
ran his fingers through the coarse thatch of his hair. "I
don't see that it matters much," he added, walking to the
hearth. "She has little to do with it."

"She has everything to do with it, and you know it very
well," retorted Morwenna. One hand was at her hip, clasping the pommel of her sword, and her eyes were bitter.
"Gwyneth could have done nothing without her—gift, if
that's what it is called, 'the Fire of The Lady.'" She spoke
with disdain. "I've already lost too many soldiers because
of what she has done, and we are threatened with war
against Kelgardh. Does that please you, Weland?"

He flinched. "You needn't say that," he murmured, pale
under the crags of his face. "I was just hoping to spare her
the grief it can bring, Mor."

"Her, or yourself?"

"Morwenna—!"

She looked down at the brick hearth. "I shouldn't have
mentioned that," she said at last. Sparks flew up and singed
her brown riding garb. "Weland, would you have come
here if nothing had happened?"

"Now, or then?"

Morwenna shook her head. "I'm no longer an infatuated student," she said, standing before the captured banners upon the wall. Her proud features were fine bronze in the light of the hearth. "I forgave you for that long ago, Weland. It left nothing worse than memories, and very few of those are even bittersweet." She smiled fondly at him. "Donal is with me, and that is your gift."

Fiona gnawed her lip in frustration. What good was all this talk? She wanted to hear more about herself. Unless it had to do with Goody Gulde. Not that she should be bothered by any of it. And there was certainly no use dawdling on the stairs now.

She saw an oaken door at the foot of the staircase, and tall racks of scrolls between it and the hearth. This was no time for hesitation. She held the railing and went down the staircase with measured steps, holding her breath. Sweat ran down the bristling nape of her neck. She carefully wiped it away, and then unlatched the door. Moonlight glazed the worn slates of a serving passage. There were no servants. Fiona quickly squeezed through the narrow opening she had permitted herself, and then eased the door shut.

A serving passage, was it? They had probably trundled her into the hall this way, hidden from sight. The main door was too good for the likes of her, no doubt!

She spat on the floor. What else could she expect from the Gentry? She recoiled from the ugly grin reflected in the windows of the passage. The face of the antlered moon gaped through her reflection. She turned and fled down the passage in denial of it. Clouds momentarily blotted up the wet moon like sponges. Fiona rubbed her eyes. She had not recognized the face in her bleak reflection. It was something that had been stripped with flensing knives. She did not look back as the sodden cloud dripped moon on the panes of glass.

The serving door was bound in straps of iron, forged to withstand siege in the Age of the Axe. Fiona turned the bolt and pushed open the massive door. The air tasted of wet pea grass and woodwash. The cobbled path before her was scrubbed clean by the wind and rain; weeds sprouted up among the worn stones. She closed the door behind her and followed the path away from Ciaran Hall.

The groves of apple and willow that bordered the estate shimmered with the lights of Lockhaven. The remaining leaves were translucent, welling up umber and yellow and pale green on dark branches. But the leaves blowing about her legs were dead and black.

Fiona ran to the gate, her boots clopping on the smooth cobblestones. Nettles and ivy smothered the gate, which was rusting on its hinges; the boughs of willows concealed most of the gray wall. She could feel the earth trembling as waves crashed at the foot of the chalk cliffs, and each breath was crisp with brine. Wizened apples crunched under her feet as she fumbled with the latch, her fingers blotched with rust. Then it was open, and she looked across the meadows that quilted together the estates of the Gentry.

The embers of a fallen star glimmered hazily in shallow pools of sweetwater, slick with rain. The fringe of reeds had soaked up most of the water. Fiona waded through the unmown heather, searching for clumps of ripe bogberries among the wet reeds, finding little more than wild turnips. She chewed on one without much appetite, although she had not eaten in three nights. She loathed turnips.

Harrow Hall could be seen in the yellow glow of lanterns that hung from five derricks. Workmen were hoisting blocks of stone and rough logs into place; apprentices carried the buckets of mortar and pitch, scrambling over flimsy scaffolds. It seemed that unearthing her sword was only part of their task. Fiona felt both pleased and oddly insulted. She was startled by the abrupt crack of muskets. In the distance burned torches, reflected in the bronze shields of the Brandwall. What had happened during her sleep? Deirdre had mentioned soldiers. —But that was not her concern. She had to worry about herself.

Lethan would certainly be unsettled when she appeared at his door. Perhaps he would not want to see her, but she would not leave until she had pocketed her gold. He could not deny her claim to it. Morning would find her on shipboard, raising sail for the Hag's Reach, or even Byrana.

Now that would be very pleasant. She would have her own cabin, its windows set with panes of yellow glass, and in the evening she would dine with the captain. She might even hire some penniless girl to be her maidservant.

Mud splashed to the knees of her breeches as she trudged through a slough of cracklecane and dead leaves. She wrinkled her nose at the rank smell that bubbled up from the depths of the mire, along with the fragile bones of birds trapped while nibbling for red-eyed springberries. Father always said that nothing but trouble came of fancifying when her mind should be on her work. Now she saw the path she should have taken, and shook her head in disgust. She had to wash before knocking at the doors of Harrow Hall.

An owl glided among flurries of black leaves, its shadow rippling coldly over puddles of rain under the hunting moon of Holdir. The stars were pale as if burning down to white ash in the wake of an immense conflagration. Fiona had never seen the night skies so empty and dark.

How many stars had fallen in the last three nights? She

looked down at her muddied garb. Let someone else worry about the heavens!

She soaked a handful of clover in the nearest puddle and wiped the mud from her breeches. Sprigs of mint would freshen the coarse homespun. It was not much, but she wanted to look tolerable, if only for herself. She was certainly not washing up for Lethan.

The cry of a falcon pierced the night, cold and sharp as an icicle. She glimpsed the whiteness of its wings, unfurling against the stars, frozen in the elegance of flight. The wet reeds crumpled mushily as she went sprawling along the edge of the puddle, her breath catching in a painful lump. She could feel the hilt of the bundled sword in her ribs, and she untied it with awkward fingers, biting her lip. The pale reflection of the falcon swept across the puddle, just under her squashed nose, but she did not sit up for long moments.

It wasn't looking for me, she decided. The wind stirred her hair, which trailed in witch's-locks from her cap, but all that she heard was the rustling of dead leaves, not the wailing of a hunter's horn. No, it wasn't looking for me, she persisted, hoping to convince herself.

A dog howled in the distance, and she wearily got to her feet. The sword glinted in her hand. She gazed numbly at it. The filigree of alder leaves smoldered with moonlight. Fiona used it to scrape the mud from her boots. There was little to be done with her clothing, which was filthier than ever now.

She frowned, listening to the night. What was that low rustling of wet reeds? It was approaching her, and it was not the wind. She gripped the sword with both hands, raising it over her shoulder, while drops of sweat trickled from her cold brow. Now a figure was limned against the smear of stars, a lantern in one hand. Fiona saw the glint of gold buttons, and then lowered the sword in relief. "Oh, for—" It was only Deirdre. "What are you doing out here?"

Deirdre raised the lantern. "I intended to ask the same of you," she said with indignation. "I can't believe that you are running away!"

The flowing honey of her hair had been drawn back with a silver comb, and she wore earrings of white gold, shaped like whelks. Her mantle was the green of damp moss, and there was silver lace at her throat; her hands were white in fingerless linen gloves, buttoned to her elbows. She looked like one of the Gentry.

"Well?" she demanded, her features impassive in the glow of the lantern. "You can't run away now! Everyone's counting upon your help! You've got to go back!"

Fiona thrust the sword into the ground, shaking her head in derision. "I know what everyone wants of me!" she snapped at Deirdre. "You can't really expect me to go back! There's nothing for me in the Three Towns!"

The older girl put down the lantern. "You can't be that thick," she said, indicating her finery with both hands. "Or do you simply enjoy being ragged and poor?"

"I'm not ashamed of it," retorted Fiona. "Nor of being from the country, which seems to be the same thing to you. I can't change simply by wearing lace and fine linen."

"Can't, or won't?"

"Won't, then!"

"You are so stubborn!" complained Deirdre. "This is an opportunity to have everything, and you want to throw it away like so much straw! You must be losing your wits! I'd give anything—!" She swallowed, and slowly unclenched her fists. "Do you truly want to lose your wits? Well, that's going to happen if you insist on running away. —Don't shake your head! Weland told me what would happen!"

"I'll take care of myself!" Fiona shouted, although she felt as if a gutting knife had been plunged into the nape of her neck. "Just leave me alone!"

Deirdre bowed her head. "Do you want to spend the rest of your days strapped down to a bed in the Abbey?" she asked angrily, her face pinched with disgust. "You'll have to eat cold gruel every morning, and endure the ceaseless groans of the others every night. You'll be gagged to stop your screaming, and led about the halls with reins." There was no pity in her unflinching eyes, gray as forgotten ash. "Do you want that?"

"It won't happen—"

"It will."

"No—no—"

"You know it will."

"Stop it!"

Deirdre clutched her mantle as dead leaves gusted out of the night. They clung to her mouth, sticky with web and soot. She choked, slapping the thick, gluey mess away with flailing hands. Her face was chalky with revulsion. She spat over and over, wiping her mouth on her elegant gloves, struggling with an urgent need to retch.

Fiona stood in numb horror. She had bitten through her lip, and blood trickled down her chin. "No!" she pleaded. "I don't want to be like this—!" Moonlight glistened icily on her brow, and embers throbbed within her head. Goody Gulde...she must have died this way, swept up in the unleashed anger that had churned inside Fiona. How many nights had she wished the goodwife dead? The puppet...even that was not spared in her hatred. Or had part of her always known just what she had done? "I have to get away!" she cried, clutching her collar tightly, as if to shut out the world. But she could no longer run away from herself. Her torn lip quivered with pain. "I can't go on like this!"

"I've got something for you," Deirdre murmured, reaching into her pocket for the silver goad. A few leaves crackled in the folds of her mantle, and fear jumped in the hollow of her throat. "H-here, take it."

"I don't know how you can even bear to look at me," said Fiona. She hesitantly took the goad, ran her fingers over the worn vines and leaves, and drew comfort from the familiar pattern. "I didn't mean to..." She knotted her thin fingers around the goad. "Do you really believe that it's best to go back?"

"It's the only thing you can do, isn't it?" Deirdre said hastily, her eyes glancing about as dogs barked across the wet fields of heather. "We shouldn't be out here all alone," she added. "Let's go back."

The smooth goad stirred up memories of childhood. "I'm glad you're my friend," said Fiona. "I *was* going to run away, and never come back. I've been running ever since my family died—" She wiped the blood from her chin. "I've got to stop doing this," she winced, licking her swollen lip. "I've got to do something..."

Deirdre picked up the lantern. "We'd better hurry," she urged. "We don't want them to come looking for us. —And don't forget your sword!" She whistled in forced admiration. "You looked very fierce with that in your hands."

"I was going to learn how to wield it," Fiona began, but she could not go on speaking of Dame Cracklecane. "I'll learn from the Marl," she said firmly, putting the precious goad in her pocket. "I'll learn everything that matters, from letters to life itself!"

Deirdre too quickly laughed. "Now that sounds more like the scourge of Balestone House! You'll probably be even worse in Ciaran Hall!"

Fiona picked up the laughter as she brushed matted reeds from her clothes. "This should annoy the laundress," she said with a grin like cracked dishes. "She'll have to scrub me to get at my clothes!"

"Several times!"

Fiona stuck out her tongue. "It's so nice of you to say

that," she added, pulling the sword from the ground. But you really shouldn't, not while this is in my hands." She giggled to smother the fears that burned like bile in her throat. "I can be very fierce," she hurried on, shaking clods of mud off the sword. "Yes, and even ferocious!"

A hunter's horn wailed in the wind, and she choked as if her voice had suddenly clotted in her throat. "Dear Lady, put out the lantern!" she managed to scream. Yet part of her was almost relieved to hear the triumphant horn. "No, it doesn't matter, not now."

Helskarth looked down at her from a long ridge of chalk and mossy boulders, the horn glinting in his hand. "Gos!" he cried, holding out his gnarled arm for the falcon. "We have caught our stray! Hasten, you sluggards! I'll not lose this one! Hasten!" He was answered by the howling of dogs. But there were no dogs.

Huntsmen stood upon the flanks of the bald ridge, scraps of old bronze mail glinting from shaggy pelts. Thongs of bear sinew were knotted about their arms from elbow to wrist; bits of bone showed in their long, single braids. Bitter years had poured strength into their lean, wiry bodies, and melted away all mercy like dross.

The white falcon came wheeling out of the darkness, its gray talons sinking into the scarred, waiting arm of the Lord of Falcondale. "We missed you, child!" He laughed, stroking the furled wings of the falcon. "You must come with me, back to Mymmorë!"

The pack of huntsmen donned heavy gauntlets, stiff with old blood and shod with claws of bronze. The cords of their taut muscles glistened with sweat and anticipation. A growl quivered eagerly in each of their throats.

Helskarth sounded the horn. The pack threw back their heads, as if tasting the wind. Then they came howling down the long flanks of the ridge, tearing at their own flesh in frenzied pursuit of their prey.

Nine

DEIRDRE FLUNG THE LANTERN, smashing it to flames in the path of the huntsmen. "Come *on!*" she urged Fiona. "The mire should also slow them—!"

The two girls ran, choking on each breath that hammered down their throats, horrified by the enraged howling at their backs. The heather was too soaked with rain for anything to burn, save the oil in the lantern. The patch of flames would be gone in moments. Then the pack of huntsmen would come on untiring legs, running across the black meadows, running them to earth under the moonlight.

The thin branches of willows dripping with wet leaves stung their faces. Fiona stumbled in the reeds and loose stones of a pond, and the heavy sword tore away from her hand. The wet air rang with the clear, merciless call of the hunter's horn, echoed and overrun by the cries of the huntsmen.

Fiona was sprawled in the reeds and bracken. "Get up!" Deirdre cried in desperation, pulling the stunned girl to her feet. "We've got to *run!*"

"I can't," Fiona sobbed, clutching the nape of her neck with cold hands. "I can't run, or move, or think straight...it hurts so much—!"

"You've got to try!" Deirdre persisted, her eyes bright with fear, blank and fragile as glass. Fiona crumpled to her knees, doubled over with cramps. "Please, before they catch up with us!"

"I'm sorry...."

Deirdre helplessly cradled the shaking girl against her breast. "Hush, don't worry," she whispered, closing her eyes to the gathering night. "It's not your fault...." She felt drops of rain on her face trickling into the hollow of her throat, fallen from the dragging boughs of the willows. There was nothing else she could do now. The cries of the huntsmen grew louder, and she tightened her arms around Fiona. "I won't let them hurt you," she said fiercely, although tears now mingled with the blotches of rain on her cheek. "I won't—!"

The thick reeds stirred wetly, and loose stones rattled under hurried footsteps. The two girls looked up uncertainly and saw Dame Cracklecane.

"You needn't be frightened," she told them, shaking out her black hair, entangled with briars and leaves. "You won't have to run away, not after this night." She knelt, drawing the bronze sword from the shallows of the pond. "I'll see to that, my dears."

A fiery crack of silver burned through the filthy reeds that clung to the sword, and clods of mud fell hissing in the pond. "I beseech You...." Dame Cracklecane closed her eyes and raised the sword with both hands. "I do not ask this for myself," she murmured. "It is for You...." The filigree of twining vines and alder leaves welled with the Fire of The Lady. It guttered with each slow breath, but it held to the blade, beating with her heart. It touched the damp air about her like spray, gleaming on her brow like sweat. "It is for You," she repeated, opening her mint-green eyes, shining with clouds of gold. "It is always for You...."

Wet leaves flew as the pack of huntsmen slashed through the grove of willows; blood dripped from their claws, running from gashes in their taut flesh. Dame Cracklecane waited in silence, her eyes unblinking, while the two girls shivered at her feet. The hunt was over. Everything was over now. The pack nodded to her and raised their claws.

Dame Cracklecane lowered the sword, smiling at the pack of huntsmen—and then the air blazed as she disembowled one of them in a hideous welter of blood and entrails, her smile undisturbed by the shuddering carcass in the reeds. Her eyes were unforgiving and cold. The only warmth in her smile was for the two girls huddled on the ground.

The pack circled her warily, their eyes flickering with hatred, their claws tearing softly, deliberately at their own flesh. There was spittle at their mouths. The air was dank with the blood and sweat trickling down the bunched sinews of their limbs.

Dame Cracklecane raised the sword, her unchanging smile harsh as the smoldering blade, her unbound hair like wisps of smoke in the wind. The pack crouched, and then flung itself upon her with slashing claws.

Ribs shattered under the sweep of the bronze sword, and the wet air was scorched; gouts of blood—not all of it that of the huntsmen—flew as if this were a pig-butchering. Howls tore the night like shards of knives. The sword crackled as if hammered out of lightning, rising and falling with the desperation of thrashing wings. Willow leaves shimmered with beads of silver fire before writhing into ash on the weeping boughs. The two girls cowered, their pallid faces splattered with blood, but neither was touched by the claws of the pack or the Fire.

It was over in horrible moments. Three of the pack lay broken in the reeds, their faces drifting with dead leaves in the pond. The rest fled through the willows. The cold wind could not wash the stench of butchery from the grove, despite the tang of brine and mint. The air was clotted with it.

Dame Cracklecane leaned on the sword. "There are worse things waiting for us," she said, clutching her side with one hand. Blood welled through her trembling fingers. "We must hurry, for there is little time left to us." She looked down at Fiona. "You've nothing to fear from me—not any longer, my dear."

She winced as the hunter's horn rang out across the wet heather, its echoes lingering in the wind. "We must be ready for them," she said, but the two girls did not stir from the bracken. "You must believe me, Fiona."

Deirdre gently folded her mantle over the trembling girl and then stopped to catch her own breath. "You can just keep away from us," she warned Dame Cracklecane. "I won't let you hurt Fiona."

Dame Cracklecane flung the sword upon the ground. "You needn't be jealous of me," she said, swallowing the bile that flooded her mouth. "It's too late for me to be her friend." Her face was ashen and lined with her years. "It's good that she has you to be her friend. Now, don't look so surprised! I can see that you have courage and strength. She'll need an abundance of both in the days ahead, and you must be the one to offer it." She suddenly closed her eyes, and her face was drenched in pain and sweat. "I didn't realize those claws had bitten so deeply—!" She smiled with effort. "I've been wounded many times, and taken worse than this, my dear. You needn't fret over it." The hunter's horn wailed harshly, and her eyes glinted angrily in the moonlight. "Helskarth calls to his fellow traitors of the Mark!"

Fiona looked up at her, clasping the silver goad in her pocket. "What do you mean?" she demanded, wiping her blurred eyes with the back of her hand. "I—I don't believe you, so it doesn't matter—just leave me *alone*—!"

"You are going to listen to me, brat!" Dame Cracklecane snapped, holding the frightened girl by her wrists. "I've

no time for pity, nor do you, not now! Helskarth already
holds the reins of the Mark. He will not rest until he holds
those of this land." She smiled bitterly, her mouth twisting
with betrayal and pain. The blood was spreading at her
side, dark as the antlers of the moon. "He has been waiting
these many years, training his packs of huntsmen, nur-
turing his traitors and his spies, waiting for us to open the
gates of Mymmorë." She tossed her black hair in anguish.
"Dear Lady, how he has used us!"

Fiona spat into the reeds. "It's all you deserve!" she cried,
her voice thick with derision. "It's different when it happens to you, isn't it! I hope it hurts!" She sobbed for breath,
tearing up handfuls of bracken. "I hope you suffer as you
made me suffer!"

Dame Cracklecane wearily bowed her head. "I have suf-
fered, and as much for you as for myself," she murmured,
clutching the boughs of a strong willow. "None of that
matters now. Helskarth is not done with you, not so long
as you possess the gift of the Fire."

"I don't *want* it!"

"You have no choice," Dame Cracklecane said, struggling to remain on her feet. "It is the one fire that can
never be quenched, unless it is by death." Bits of leaves
slipped through her fingers, and she twisted the wet
branches about her trembling hand. "It is burning within
you, and if it is not set within wards, it will burn until there
is nothing left of you but a witless husk. Now that is the
truth, and you know it, my dear."

Fiona put her hands to her ears. "I don't want to hear
any of this!" she screamed, her face plastered with filth
and lank strands of hair. "Go *away*—!"

"Helskarth craves your power, and he would just as soon
find you witless, unable to defy him." The branches bit
deeply into her flesh as she sagged from the willows. "He
will put you in chains and he will seek to bend you under

his will—just as he seeks to do with poor Elspeth." She shuddered as more blood ran from her side, and her face turned chalky, but she would not falter now. "He is hunting her, just as he is hunting you, child. And he will surely catch you, unless you have mastered the Fire. You must believe me, for it is your only hope, Fiona."

"Why is this happening to me?" Fiona pleaded, unable to ignore these insistent words. "It hurts... I don't want it to happen...."

"It won't, not if you allow yourself to trust me," Dame Cracklecane said, her eyes clouded with grief. "Or would you rather be carted off mewling to the dungeons of Falcondale?"

Fiona wearily shook her head. "I—I don't know what to do," she murmured, her hands loose and cold in her lap. "I'm tired...." Her voice trickled away in sweat. But she would not succumb. "I can't trust you, but—" She sat up straight in the dank bracken. There was pain in her eyes, but it was that of struggling with herself. She pulled her fingers into small fists. "I'll have to take that risk."

"No!" Deirdre cried, the pale gray of her eyes cracking like sheets of ice. The fears that surfaced were rotted with years of hiding and moved in her eyes like dead things. "I won't let you! She's lying! You can't trust her! You can't trust—" She covered her mouth, fingers stabbing clumsily across her lips, as if she could not feel them. "Oh, do what you want!" she muttered, wiping her nose. "It's always what you want, isn't it?"

Fiona lowered her head. "I don't know what you want of me," she said quietly. "I just want to stay *me*, and any risk is worth that, isn't it?"

"I suppose so," Deirdre said, fiddling with the buttons of her elegant gloves. She wound a loose thread about one of her bare fingers, unwilling to stop even when the fine linen began to unravel in her hand. "Well, go ahead!"

Dame Cracklecane settled among the reeds, spreading the folds of her kirtle on the ground. "Come, sit with me," she said warmly, gathering up the twigs and leaves that clung to her hems. "Come, my dear."

Fiona crawled into her lap, flinching at the blood that soaked one side of the kirtle. The hunting horn wailed over the wet fields of heather, and the hesitant girl clutched at Dame Cracklecane. The sagging boughs of the willows dripped rainwater on their faces, and the green leaves shone quietly in the moonlight. The pond trembled with ripples, but there was no wind. The air tasted of apple blossoms, mossy waters shaded by chestnut, and stones baked under the sun; beads of silver fire glistened on reeds, twigs, pebbles, and tufts of withered linsey. Fiona closed her eyes. She could feel the slow throbbing of the Fire.

Deirdre pulled away, more from angry compulsion than any wariness of the power stirring about her, which she felt like the mounting tautness of the air before a summer storm.

Dame Cracklecane was shaping runes out of the twigs and leaves gathered from her kirtle. Each was misted with silver fire as she flung it upon the ground, casting a rough circle around the two of them. "Root and leaf, branch and blossom," she chanted, dipping one hand in the pond. "Her womb brings forth life, and all that lives, and all that is of this earth about us: all honor to Her." She let the pond water trickle from her hand over Fiona. The air was quivering like a drawn bow, rustling the boughs of the willows, but there was still no wind. "There is only The Lady."

Deirdre sat in the thick bracken, elbows resting on her knees, and chin balanced on her knuckles. She was horrified to feel tears running down her cheeks as she looked at Fiona and Dame Cracklecane.

"I don't care," she muttered, grinding the heels of her

boots into the ground. The harsh cry of a scarly was suddenly hungry with loneliness. She should have expected it. "It's not so dreadful."

She swallowed the desperate lie with the bile it raised in her throat. It made her ill, for she felt that she would lose Fiona. She had never felt this longing for others, not even her parents. Deirdre supposed that her mother had cared for her once, but she could not remember it. She refused to try. Fiona was the only one she had ever cared for since her loathed childhood. She was frightened at the depths of her longing, but she could not deny it.

She dug furrows in the earth with her heels. There had to be some fairness in the world, and not the shoddy kind for which she had settled all her life. She had settled for too much already, and she was sick of it.

Deirdre frowned. Her tears were drying up like ghosts. She wiped away their traces with her sleeve. Her stepfather had taught her the futility of tears. What use ever came of them?

The fallen sword glinted in the reeds. She reached for its hilt. The knobs of bone and gold felt greasy to her damp fingers, and the blade ran with blood. She cleaned the fine bronze with a handful of wet bracken. It was something to do for Fiona.

The hunter's horn sounded once more, drawing closer and louder with each note, but it was not the call to the pack of huntsmen. It was a thin, boneless wail, and its echoes were shriveled things, lost in the night. Dame Cracklecane looked up in horror.

"What's wrong?" Fiona said drowsily, clutching the goad in her pocket. She felt as if her muscles had turned to cold porridge. "I feel something—dark—so dark..."

Dame Cracklecane hugged the shivering girl close to her breast. "You mustn't be frightened," she whispered, although her own face was ashen with more than her wounds. "Once the wards have been set, you shall wield the Fire."

"It's coming closer—"

"It's nothing, my dear."

"No!" Fiona insisted, sitting up as dead leaves drifted out of the night. "Can't you feel it? There's something out there—!"

Dame Cracklecane furiously clutched her by the locks of her hair. "Now you listen to me!" she said, her voice shrill with desperation. "I've endured too much for you to muck it all up now! You've been chosen by The Lady! That's all that matters to me, so stop whining and do as you're told, do you hear?"

Fiona angrily yanked her hair loose, wiping her eyes on the sleeve of her patched jacket. "I shouldn't have listened to you that first night!" she fumed, knowing that she needed the woman. "I'm not doing this for you, *or* for your precious Lady! It's for *me,* so hurry up! And don't you dare pull my hair again!"

The air was mottled with dead leaves, which stuck to their faces with runes of web and soot. Fiona clawed them off with squeamish fingers, unable to bear their touch. They felt like wet moths.

The wail of the hunter's horn swept through the rustling of leaves, pitiless as the moon. The calling of her name was its answer. "Fiona...?"

She went gray at that voice, and looked up at the woman in the boughs of the willows. The shadows of leaves trembled on the dark green apron dotted wtih marigolds; beads of silver fire clung to the folds of the plain brown kirtle. Hair like heaps of straw was gathered in a loose bun. The air dripped with the sweetish odor of the plague, and the pale reeds were black with the imprint of bare feet.

Fiona saw only the round face, stiff and white as birch

bark. "Mama?" she said uncertainly, her voice dwindling away to little more than babyish years. Dame Cracklecane clasped her arm. "Let go of me!" she yelled, prying the weak fingers off like leeches. But her anger quickly guttered out as she looked at the woman in the willows. "You can't be—you," she said, but the desperate need to believe drowned her wits and distrust. "I've wanted you for so long—" The words cracked in her throat. "You'd never let anything happen to me," she went on, fumbling with her limp hands. "I knew you wouldn't, I just knew it!"

"I'm here now," said the woman, her dark eyes glittering from the moony stillness of her face. "You needn't be afraid any longer. I'll care for you again. Now, wouldn't you like that, Fiona?"

"Yes," she answered. "Oh, yes!"

"You need only take my hand," said the woman, smoothing her kirtle with impatient fingers. "Come, and it will all be over, my child."

Fiona struggled to her feet. The dead leaves no longer fell, although the pond was scummed over with them. "It will all be over," she murmured, understanding the runes upon the leaves at last. What else had she ever wanted? — But not like this! The denial screamed from deep within her, frightening her into hesitation. She felt the doubts buzzing like midges in the back of her mind. How could this woman really be her mother?

"Daddy isn't here," she said, strength returning to her voice despite bitter chills and cramps. Sweat trickled down her confused face, leaving pale lines in the filth and dried blood that encrusted it. "Why isn't he with you, Mama?"

"He is waiting for you," said the woman, stepping among the reeds. Moonlight curdled in her eyes, and the patches of reeds were matted with decay under her feet. "You shouldn't keep him waiting, Fiona."

Dame Cracklecane drew herself up in the bracken. "Your

father is dead!" she cried, her fingers sinking into her deep wounds. "He's dead, Fiona! And so is your mother! That is nothing but her corpse, given the mockery of life through the Fire!"

"You mustn't listen to her lies!" hissed the woman, her fingers clawing the air like dead twigs. "She has been lying to you all along, and she is lying now!"

Fiona clasped her throbbing head. "I saw you buried in the heather of the Haugh," she moaned, twisting her scarf into knots. "I sold the good copper kettle and the linen napkins to buy a headstone for you and Daddy. —Oh, this is witless! I can't believe we're talking of such things! I can't believe any of this!"

The woman held out her hands. "I am your mother," she said, wisps of flaxen hair trailing on her cheeks. "You can believe in me, Fiona."

"I want to—"

"Come with me, and everything can be just as it was, my dearest. The family can be together once more, just you and me and Daddy. We can forget that anything bad ever happened to us. That's what you want, isn't it?"

"You're *dead....*"

"Daddy is carving a new pair of ice skates for you, and you can help me pick bogberries for a cobbler. Now, wouldn't that be nice?"

"Please, don't—"

"We've decided to buy you the horse you wanted for your twelfth birthday. Daddy wanted to surprise you, but we can't have you pining away for that long! How would you fancy one of those spotted grays from Neat Spinney?"

"Stop it—!"

The woman drew closer, until she stood before the circle of runes in the bracken. The odor of plague was overwhelming in its sweetness of decay. The runes flickered hesitantly at her barren feet.

"Do you mean to forget your family?" she said, the holes of her eyes seething darkness. "Do we mean so little to you, Fiona?"

"No, no, *no—!*"

"Enough!" Dame Cracklecane demanded, wrapping her mantle about the girl. Silver blazed angrily upon her brow, although she barely had the strength to raise her head. "I shall burn your wretched corpse to ashes! You won't claim this child for the Mark!"

"She is my child."

Deirdre spat into the pond. The bronze sword gleamed in her gloved hands. "Leave her alone, you horrible thing!" she screamed, plunging the sword into the woman. "Just leave her *alone!*"

The woman sank to the earth with an agonized wail, blood spurting foul and black from her writhing shoulders. Deirdre thrust the sword even deeper, as if skewering a beetle with a long pin, her eyes blind as buttons. The woman thrashed upon the ground. Deirdre shuddered, but she did not let go of the sword. Spatters of blood withered the bracken. The limbs of the woman grew still. Deirdre covered her mouth and stumbled away in horror.

Fiona numbly shook her head. This could not possibly be her mother. "It isn't real," she whispered, struggling not to shriek. But the face was plain as milk. "It's not—!"

Dame Cracklecane opened her arms with the silence of deep invocation. "Dear Lady, my beloved, forgive what must be done for You."

Fiona squirmed as she felt trembling fingers press like icicles into the nape of her neck. "No, don't—" And then it was as if an iron spike drawn hot from the forge had been plunged into her flesh and burst into molten splinters within her head.

Deirdre clung to the willows. Their thin boughs cut into her fingers as a storm of dead leaves raged through the hollow. The runes of web and soot were turned to blood, and the air burned cold and white as foaming water, radiant with the Fire.

Fiona stood in the ferns and reeds, hair blowing in the tumult of leaves, silver misting her brow. She slowly raised her arms to the trees, tendrils of silver fire cupped in her hands. The air was pungent, as if a meadow of wild thyme and fennel had been plowed up and the damp earth scattered with cloves; withered branches began to swell with green buds, and silver dew glistened in the fronds of bracken. Fiona spread her fingers, and the veins of countless leaves seemed to burn across her hands. But her eyes were emptied inward, dark as the ocean, and she lolled in the arms of Dame Cracklecane.

The woman was pale as she fashioned the wards that must shield and sustain Fiona. The moon slid like melting snow in her eyes, dwindling into gray slush, and blood poured out of her side to cloud the Fire. She was drawing upon the deepest wellsprings of her power to set the intricate wards, knowing that it would mean her death. She could feel the coldness in her heart. It would squeeze the breath out of her body, but she would not falter in this last offering of her devotion to The Lady.

Fiona was mantled in silver mist, and sparks of hot gold stirred in her tangled hair, redolent of sage and yarrow. As the radiance gathered upon her brow, strength flooded through her limbs. She could feel the weaving of the wards, delicate as a fledgling's down, strong as the roots of mountains.

Now the swirling black leaves rushed into the depths of the autumn sky, blotting out the still moon in their rustling flight. Dame Cracklecane smiled as she crumpled to the dark ground.

"I'm done," she whispered, her eyes growing pale as the matted reeds that cushioned her head. She struggled for each breath, feeling as if huge stones were being heaped upon her chest. "It is for You...."

"This isn't how you wanted it to be, is it?" Fiona said helplessly as she knelt by the woman. "I wasn't the girl that you wanted me to be, that's the trouble. I never even cared about The Lady."

There was no Fire. She was a skinny girl, bundled up in an old jacket, her freckles smeared with dirt. "I would have cared about you," she said gently, twisting her floppy cap in her hands. "Why couldn't that have been enough?"

"I wanted you to be my daughter...My very own...." Dame Cracklecane painfully gasped out each word. "It was wrong of me...but no child would ever quicken in my womb. I could not let you go...."

"It wasn't so wrong," Fiona said, touching the cold lips of the woman with concern. "Hush. Don't talk. I'll have to get a barber—" She shut her eyes to the hideous wound. The country ministrations of a barber were suited for little more than croup and broken limbs. "I've got to do something," she persisted. "Tell me—"

"It doesn't matter...."

"It does!" Fiona cried, wisps of silver fire smoldering upon her brow. "I don't want you to die! I'll need you with me, helping me—!" She struggled not to sob. "Everything's all churned up inside of me. I can't get through any of this by myself. You can't die, you just can't!"

"Lethan—tell him—"

Dame Cracklecane dug her fingers into the ground, as if wracked with pain. Her eyes grew dull, fading with quiet inevitability. The breath went out of her with an agonized cry: "My Lady!" Her fingers grew limp, and the pain was smoothed from her worn face, now dappled with the shadows of leaves and moonlight.

Fiona rose to her feet. "I'm sorry," she said, but the words sounded cold and hollow. What else could she say?

The words were always the same, like so many tin ornaments. One was expected to display them. Yet she felt an
aching need to say something. "I hope that you'll find your
Lady—"

"Look out!" screamed Deirdre.

Fiona turned, her eyes numb. "Please, no...." The body
of her mother slowly lifted its head. The face leered at her
in the glow of the Fire. Bony fingers reached back to wrench
the impaling sword loose, and rivulets of foulness oozed
from the wound. The odor of plague filled the air as the
ungainly figure rose to its feet.

"You mustn't turn away from me," said the woman, tossing the sword down in the reeds. The round face was
mottled with decay. "I'm here for you, Fiona. Don't you
want to see your kind, loving Mama?"

"You aren't my mother!" Fiona said, her witch's-locks of
hair glinting with sparks of gold. Bile and anger soured
her mouth. "You're just an ugly thing that serves the Mark!"
It sickened her to look upon this mockery of her mother,
and she welcomed the flood of the Fire. "I've had my fill
of you and your filthy kind!"

The mouth gaped with laughter as brittle as the scratch-
ing of chalk on slate. "You sound like poor Gwynnie! She
didn't have the stomach to do what must be done for the
Mark! We've come too far to be stopped now, least of all
by an unlettered child!"

Fiona choked on the taunt. "You aren't *anything* like my
mother!" she cried, her voice shaking as if she had just
been birched. "She wouldn't *ever* say those awful things!"
She was shrieking now. "You—witchwife!"

"You pitiful little dunce!" The air cackled with more
laughter from the woman. "You are scarcely one to be
calling others *that*, my lambkin! Dear me, but you are even
more of a thickwit than you look! You are surely too lump-
ish to be a threat to the Mark!"

"You—you—" Fiona struggled for her voice, snatching up the fallen sword from the reeds. "I'll show you who's the thickwit!"

She lunged furiously toward the woman, sinking the blade deep between the sagging breasts. Fire cracked in a writhing lash of silver that blazed down the length of the sword. The hideous wound bubbled with decay and stench. Yet the rotting teeth were bared in a cruel grin.

Fiona shuddered as the wards of her power were suddenly besieged by the gathered wills of the Mark. Her hands seemed stuck to the sword, and she dimly realized that she had been goaded into her enraged attack. Thickwit! What good was her power without the knowledge to wield it? She could not hope to resist the full strength of the Mark!

No! She would not yield, although her clenched fingers were already starting to blister, and her temples throbbed as if they would burst. There must be some way to resist their might!

Drops of blood ran in the vines and leaves cut into the bronze, hissing like grease in the Fire. The odor of plague mingled with that of spent lightning. Fiona chewed upon her lip as pain washed through her thin body.

She could not hope to match the overwhelming power that flowed from the Mark. Stone would shatter at its touch. But if she could destroy the vessel through which that power was flowing, would that be enough?

The agonized face that loomed through her blurred eyes answered her doubts. She clasped the sword more tightly, her knuckles white with pain and determination. The air tasted of wet mint through the decay. Fiona desperately plunged the sword even deeper, ignoring the pain that was grinding away the bones of her fingers, seeing the wards that protected her like runes of leaves and twigs in her mind. She could feel the power welling up within her, and she directed it clumsily but inexorably through the sword.

The body of her mother writhed like a hooked eel on the blade, its dry fingers snapping off with each useless blow of its hands. "Stop it!" the woman pleaded, struggling to pull away from the mounting blaze of the Fire. "You would destroy your own mother—!"

"You *aren't* my mother!"

"Fiona, listen to me—"

"I won't!"

"I was dead, and the spark of life was rekindled by the Mark! I had no choice but to serve them! You must listen to me, for only you can save me, my dearest!"

"You're lying!"

"I beg you, release me from this slavery!" The mottled eyes ran with sluggish tears. "Do you loathe me so much? Do you long to see me suffer, Fiona?"

The silver fire gusted hesitantly along the edge of the sword. Fiona painfully tossed her head, unable to go through this again. It simply could not be her mother! — But what if it was, and not some ogress raised up by the Mark? She *would* be destroying her own mother— "No!"

Deirdre swallowed the bile rising in her throat. "You mustn't listen to her lies!" she cried, cowering in the thick reeds. "You said that you didn't want to be treated like a witless child! You can't go on living like one! You have to grow up!" Her voice broke with desperation. "Fiona, she's already *dead*—!"

The sword quivered in tightening hands. "You're dead," Fiona whispered, looking into the face of the truth. "You're dead!" The grove of willows blazed with silver fire for one blinding moment. The bond was severed between her mother and the Mark. All bonds were severed now. "I want to live!"

The corpse had wrenched itself from the sword, stumbling to its knees in the wet reeds. Tongues of silver fire burned angrily within its eyes and mouth. The loose bun of hair was all that remained of the woman who had been buried months ago in the Haugh.

"I also want to live—" The splintered stumps of its fingers pawed the air, reeking of decay. "You want to see me die!"

The face began to wither, and ash blew from the rotting bones of its cheeks. Fiona shuddered but could not look away as the crumbling figure lurched to its feet. Blood ran like honey from its mouth, sluggish and black. The air was bitter as iron.

"How can you do this...?" Fiona swallowed, and her wan eyes were those of a trapped hare. "Dear Lady—" The corpse splashed blindly into the pond. Its flailing hands clutched at the reeds. "I beseech You...." The green apron floated on the water like scum. Fiona could see the yellow stitches of the marigolds. The corpse slipped beneath the cold water, and the silver fire guttered out, leaving the moon to tremble in the pond. Fiona closed her eyes, but she still saw the yellow marigolds. She would always see them.

The hunter's horn wailed in the silence, dwindling over the meadows. She opened her eyes. The willows sighed in the moonlight. The shadows of leaves drifted in the pond.

Fiona lowered the sword. The soothing trill of crickets wrapped her like a warm blanket. The lonely breeze tasted of the sea as it brushed her moving lips. She was struggling to sing an old lullaby, but she could not recall the words. All she could do was murmur the tune with each ragged breath.

There were no tears on her freckled cheeks. She was all cried out. What were the words to that lullaby? She did not even remember its name. It was gone, like her family and her childhood.

She combed thin fingers through her witch's-locks. What was she supposed to do with her life now? Muskets cracked in the distance, reminding her of the world. She could not turn away from it.

Father would have told her to set her life in order, and then get on with it. She smiled despite herself. His advice was always good, as he would be the first to boast. Not that he was a braggart. He was simply Daddy.

Why wasn't he here when she needed him? She clasped the cattle goad in her pocket. He was dead. Nothing could bring him back. He was dead.

What of the Fire? She did not want him brought back as her mother had been, enslaved and defiled by the Mark. Never that way! Let him remain in the Haugh. Why couldn't the world leave her family alone? But it had not. Nor would it leave her alone.

Fiona would not run away from it. She would grow up and stop being that foolish little girl. She would take her place as head of the family. There was only her great-aunt and two cousins, one in the mills and one in the ranks, but it was her family. Father would want her to hold them together, and she understood that being without any family had been as crippling for her as losing one of her limbs.

Deirdre walked up beside her in the moonlight. "They'll probably be looking for us, so let's go back to the Hall," she urged, wiping her mouth with a handful of willow leaves. She had been horribly ill, and the color returning to her face was blotched. "You're going back with me, aren't you?" Her eyes darted with fear. "You've just got to, Fiona! They won't let me stay there all by myself! I know they won't! And I don't want to go back to the orphanage! I'd rather be a drudge in a workhouse!" She abruptly bit her tongue. "I'll be gibbering next," she said, smoothing her mantle with unsteady hands. "I won't go back to the orphanage, that's all. I can't go back, not after all that's happened; I'd rather be dead first." She was in control of herself now. "I'd like to stay with you at the Hall, if you don't take any disliking to it. They'll have to do as you say, after all."

Fiona laughed curtly. "Yes—and country girls shouldn't go to town by themselves, anyway!" She had heard that leering joke often enough. "We'll stay together—we're friends!"

Deirdre smiled to herself. "I'm going to start bawling my eyes out like some goosy girl," she murmured, steepling her fingers and pressing them to her lips. "Let's never quarrel! Let's always be best friends!"

"Well, of course we will!" Fiona said, hugging the older girl about the waist. "You really are goosy if you don't know that! —Now, there's just one more thing that needs doing, and then we'll go back."

"Very well."

Fiona hefted the bronze sword, walking through the reeds to the crumpled figure of Dame Cracklecane. "You deserved far better than this from your Lady," she whispered, leaning down to close the wide eyes that reflected the willow leaves blowing in the wind. "And you deserved better from me, as well. But that's just spoiled milk now. It should be thrown away." Her father always said that was better than to dwell upon regrets. She would be like him.

She used her sword to dig the simple grave, wrapped the body in its mantle of star-gold, and covered it with branches of willow. The clumps of earth were gently set in place, and it was done. There was no headstone, but that did not trouble the girl. Here were root and leaf, branch and blossom. Dame Cracklecane needed nothing more. Fiona wiped her hands on her breeches and walked away from the mound.

She stopped at the edge of the pond. It was strewn with dead reeds, floating like yellowish locks of hair. She closed her eyes, clasping the goad in her pocket. The memories were muddied now.

Deirdre carefully touched her arm. "You didn't have any other choice," she said, looking away from the still waters of the pond. "I know if it had been *my* mother—" She spat in the reeds. "It wasn't your fault."

"I wouldn't let her rest at all," Fiona said, taking the goad from her pocket. She ran one finger over the filigree of twining vines and leaves, black with the gathering years. "I wouldn't let either of them rest—and as for the Mark..." It was painful to go on, and she bit her lip. "They did nothing that I hadn't done already, in my own way. I kept them alive, and went on being a little girl. I couldn't let go. —But you have to let go!" she cried, and abruptly threw the cattle goad into the pond. "You've got to go on with your own life. And I'm going to go on with mine."

"You didn't have to do that!" Deirdre said, watching the rippling water grow smooth. "Weland told me that it could be older than Therrilyn! How are you going to get it back?"

Fiona looked up at the fixed stars gleaming through the white and gold mist. "It doesn't matter," she said. "I don't want it back." The moving stars swarmed like midges. "There are things you simply have to leave behind."

Deirdre fidgeted in the soggy reeds. "Well, that's the best thing," she said hastily, looking about the hollow. "We can go now."

"I suppose we should," Fiona said, her smile crooked as a witch's divining branch. "I need a thorough scrubbing, and a warm bed, and lots of sleep." But she waited, her fingers tightening on the hilt of her sword. "Do you hear that?" she demanded as the cry of a falcon blew tauntingly in the wind. "They made me feel like something eaten by maggots." Deirdre flinched at her words. The willows stirred uncomfortably in the moonlight. "As for the Mark—!" Fiona clasped the blade of her sword. She chanted a child's curse as blood trickled from her hand. The blade cut deeply, but that did not matter to her. "*This* for the Mark—!"

Drops of blood were flung into the night. "I'll set my words against all of their prophecies," Fiona said, wringing the pain from her hand. "We'll see what turns to ashes, and what turns to gold."

She looked at her sword. The filigree of alder leaves dripped redly in the moonlight. "Let my blood call for their blood," she said harshly. "Let them suffer as they made me suffer—!"

"Do you have to go on like that?" Deirdre asked, hoping to make an uncomfortable joke out of it. "They must be worse than Goody Gulde!"

Fiona slowly lowered the sword. The warm bitterness of blood in the air soured each breath. "Goody Gulde," she said at last. She had always loathed the woman. She felt little sadness at her death. But she never wanted to be responsible for that death. It had festered within her, until she could no longer ignore it. And she realized that some things could never be left behind.

"No," she murmured, squeezing drops of blood from her fist. "I don't have to go on like a thickwit." She laughed brokenly to herself. Goody Gulde had finally taught her a lesson. She wiped her fingers on her jacket. "There's been enough blood shed for one night."

The lonely cries of gulls chilled the air, piercing her to the heart. She had not chosen the power she bore, but she could choose the responsibility of it. She remembered that evening on the cliff, listening to the gulls. She had chosen to accept her life then, no matter how difficult. She would accept it now.

The stars were ebbing, but their dim trails lingered in silver and cinnamon. Fiona sighed, for the morning would not be pleasant. Lethan should be told of all that had happened this night. The nonsense that she had concocted as an excuse for running away would have been easier, and it would hardly have troubled the Marl. The gold did not matter to him. All that mattered was Jennet.

Fiona stirred up ripples in the pond. There was a wisp of blood trailing from her sword, but the water soon smoothed itself like an ironed bedsheet. The blade glistened cleanly in the moonlight. She sighed once more, for the ripples that would spread from this night seemed endless, and she did not believe they would ever grow smooth. They would simply cause more ripples, and on, and on....

But that was not her concern. There would be more than enough for her to do with her gift. Dame Cracklecane would be depending upon her to deal with the Mark. She would have to talk with Weland. She smiled weakly. There was so much to be done! —But she was willing to do it. And she needed no oath to bind her to the task. She was her father's daughter. That was pledge enough for a flock of Marls!

Fiona smiled grimly to herself in the pond. "Well, don't just stand there!" she said, turning to Deirdre. "Let's be on our way to Ciaran Hall!"